No matter what else he was doing. Their eyes would meet, and then he'd go back to refilling glasses, joking with the girls or watching a recap of the day's football highlights.

Her skin prickled with excitement. They were going to be alone tonight. She knew what that might mean, and judging by the quick intake of his breath whenever they came close, so did he.

Ever since she'd seen Zack standing in front of the third-grade classroom a couple of months ago, Jan had longed to touch him all over. She couldn't stop now, even though her instincts warned that she'd be running a risk. If this relationship blew up in their faces, their delicate balance over Kimmie's upbringing might shatter.

*No matter how much caution I've learned, I'm still impulsive.* And this particular impulse refused to be ignored....

Dear Reader,

At Safe Harbor Medical Center, the next step after establishing the new fertility center is to set up an egg donor program. This book introduces Jan Garcia, RN, former fiancée of an obstetrician who's appeared in several previous books in the series. She's just arrived to head up the program, with which Dr. Zack Sargent is closely involved.

He has a big surprise in store.

There's a natural tension and attraction between these former lovers, who parted eight years earlier. Jan was unfairly accused of harming a patient and Zack believed the charges. Furious, Jan threw his ring at him.

When she discovered she was pregnant, he signed papers so she could relinquish the baby for adoption. Although Jan had a change of heart, she never told him she kept little Kimmie. After all, by the time she was cleared of charges, he was already engaged to someone else.

Now she's back in town, and they both have to face their shared parentage. Zack, a widower, must connect with the daughter Jan kept from him all these years. And he has to do that without hurting his adopted stepdaughter, who's only a year older than Kimmie.

How can two wounded and very different people work together, professionally and personally? Especially when, against their better judgment, they're falling in love again? Welcome to their story!

Jacqueline Diamond

# The M.D.'s
# Secret Daughter

## JACQUELINE DIAMOND

**HARLEQUIN**®

entertain, enrich, inspire™

Recycling programs
for this product may
not exist in your area.

ISBN-13: 978-0-373-75424-3

THE M.D.'S SECRET DAUGHTER

Copyright © 2012 by Jackie Hyman

www.Harlequin.com

**Printed in U.S.A.**

## ABOUT THE AUTHOR

Writing about a fertility program at a medical center draws on Jackie's longstanding interest in medicine, her own fertility treatments (result: two terrific sons, now in their twenties) and her skill, as a former Associated Press reporter, in researching the latest developments in the field. An author of ninety romances, mysteries, Regencies and paranormals, Jackie lives in Orange County, California, with her husband of more than thirty years. You can visit Jackie at www.jacquelinediamond.com and follow her on Twitter @jacquediamond. Thanks!

### Books by Jacqueline Diamond

#### HARLEQUIN AMERICAN ROMANCE

In Memory of Dr. Bonnie Hock Lamar

# Chapter One

"If I can't have a kitten," said Kimmie, "how about a daddy?"

Jan Garcia, R.N., nearly spit her morning coffee into the windshield. She quickly swallowed, grateful the car was stopped at a red light. Of all the concerns on her mind this morning, how had her seven-year-old daughter managed to hit on the one that troubled Jan most?

Returning her cup to its holder, she regarded the girl belted into the passenger seat beside her. Intense frown lines puckered Kimmie's forehead beneath straight dark bangs. Uh-oh. She'd seized on a theme and her daughter had the tenacity of a bulldog.

First tactic: make light of the matter. "You're kidding, right?"

"Fiona has a daddy. She used to live with just him and no mommy," Kimmie said earnestly. "I bet he'll bring her to school today."

"And I'm bringing you." This morning she'd pressed Kimmie's pink blouse and the ruffle on the pink-and-tan skirt, and applied a curling iron to her daughter's long dark hair, the same color as Jan's. Still, a little girl couldn't be expected to appreciate how much love her mommy lavished on her.

"Now Fiona has a daddy *and* a mommy," Kimmie continued stubbornly. "Why can't I have both?"

When the light changed, Jan eased the car forward. Thank goodness she was driving through a quiet section of Safe Harbor, because she had to force herself to focus.

*That's what I get for trying to do the right thing.* Concerned about how her daughter would adjust to starting second grade at a new school—they'd recently relocated from Texas to California—Jan had made a point of getting together last weekend with an old friend and coworker, embryologist Alec Denny, his new wife, Patty, and his six-year-old daughter. Even though Fiona was a year younger, Jan thought knowing a girl at the new school might help soothe Kimmie's anxiety.

Good intentions didn't always work out as expected. She should have remembered daddies had become a frequent topic of discussion since Kimmie read a book about a girl finding her father.

Next tactic: change the subject. "I'm sorry you can't have a kitten at our apartment. I promise to look for a place that accepts pets. But I'm starting a new job, so it may take a while."

"I miss my kitties." A world of sadness laced the little girl's voice, making Jan sorry she'd switched to such a painful topic.

"We were only fostering those kittens till they could find good homes," she reminded her daughter.

Big green eyes regarded her hopefully. "We can do that here."

"No pets means no pets. Not even foster kittens." To her right, between two-story stucco buildings, Jan glimpsed the small harbor that gave the town its name. "Look. Isn't that pretty?"

"Huh." Moodily, Kimmie shifted the backpack on her lap and stared straight ahead.

*She'll adjust.* Maybe if Jan repeated that about a dozen times, she'd believe it herself.

When world-renowned fertility expert Dr. Owen Tartikoff, Jan's former boss from a previous job in Boston, offered her a position as head of the new egg-donor program at Safe Harbor Medical Center, she'd leaped at the chance. She'd be working with a top-notch medical team that included some old friends.

Another factor in moving West was being close to family. Jan had grown up half an hour's drive from here in Santa Ana, where her mother, brother, sister-in-law and two nieces lived. Her mother had even volunteered to pick Kimmie up after school whenever Jan needed her.

There was one major drawback. Jan preferred not to think about him right now. Okay, if she weren't in total denial, she would have contacted Dr. Zack Sargent as soon as she saw his name on the hospital's staff roster. But what did you say to the man who'd dumped you when you needed him most and married someone else while you were still hurting? *By the way, I didn't give up our baby for adoption like I said I would, so get over it?*

Sooner or later, Jan would have to tell him the truth. When she did, she could picture Zack getting all rigid and judgmental; he was good at that. She doubted he'd want to be a part of their lives and, although that posed problems in its own way, she was glad.

Kimmie didn't need a reluctant daddy. She didn't need to play second fiddle to Zack's wife and any kids they'd had in the intervening years. Jan didn't intend to let him break Kimmie's heart the way he'd broken hers.

All the same, she dreaded the inevitable confrontation. If she'd been smart, she'd have let him know about Kimmie while they were still safely in Texas, and while she had time to change her mind about the move. How come she was so good at planning her professional life and so lousy at dealing with her personal one?

She drove past the stucco Civic Center buildings and joined a line of cars inching into the elementary school's parking lot. When Jan enrolled Kimmie last week, the assistant principal had given her a map. Arranged like a fork with three detached prongs, the school's low white buildings lay between City Hall Park and the middle school.

As the car rolled forward Jan grumbled under her breath about an oversize vehicle hogging an extra space. Mercifully, she found an empty one, although it was a tight squeeze for her red sedan.

"Got everything?" she asked as she cut the engine. She'd downloaded a list of recommended supplies from the school's website and checked it twice. Still, in the stress of preparing for her first day at work, as well as the start of school, she might have overlooked something. "Paper? Pencils, markers and glue? Lunch?"

"Mischief," Kimmie said as she shrugged on her backpack.

Her door half-open, Jan hesitated in confusion. Then she noted the well-worn teddy bear in her daughter's grip. The school encouraged students in the early grades to bring a favorite stuffed animal on opening day.

"Absolutely. We can't forget Mischief." Chuckling at her misunderstanding, Jan got out, smoothed her tailored aqua dress and straightened the matching jacket.

Parents and kids, the smaller ones also toting stuffed animals, streamed toward the buildings while cars continued prowling for spaces. The website had advised parents to use the middle-school lot—classes didn't start there until tomorrow—or park a block away at the community center. *Busy day for everybody,* Jan reflected, grateful she'd found a spot so close.

In the distance she glimpsed Fiona clutching a panda on one side and her stepmother's hand on the other. Alec prowled alongside, video-camera recording his daughter's arrival for the start of first grade. To Jan's relief, Kimmie was too short to see them through the crowd.

At moments like this, she wished her daughter had a loving father. *Not just at moments like this, either.* Maybe someday Jan would meet the right guy. After all, she was only thirty.

Resolutely, she turned her attention to the map. Mrs. Humphreys's second-grade classroom lay at the end of the right-hand building, and there it was, straight ahead.

In the doorway stood a smartly dressed woman a little taller than Jan's five foot three, her broad features warm with welcome as she greeted a blond boy and patted his green dinosaur. "Brady? I'm delighted to have you in my class this year."

"Me, too," he said in a high voice, speaking as the dinosaur. "I'm Sneezer."

The boy's mother, hanging on to a little girl, added playfully, "He packed plenty of tissues in case Sneezer starts snuffling."

"Meeting everyone's stuffed animals is fun. We'll take a class picture that I'll post on my web page. It's downloadable." Glancing at Jan, the teacher said, "Hi, I'm Paula Humphreys."

"Jan Garcia." She ushered Kimmie forward. "We just moved here from Houston, so this is quite a change for Kimmie."

"For Mischief, too," the girl added solemnly.

"I'm sure you'll both feel at home very soon." The teacher indicated a wall of photos inside the classroom, depicting raccoons, brown bears, opossums, bobcats, coyotes, skunks and other native wildlife. "As you can see, I love animals."

"Me, too!" Brightening, Kimmie hurried inside, holding up her teddy so it could see the pictures.

Jan retreated to make room for new arrivals. Although her mothering instinct urged her to stay, it would be best to leave while her daughter was occupied. Besides, she faced her own challenges this morning.

As she walked toward the parking lot, Brady's mother, a short brunette with a warm smile, fell into step. Jan slowed to accommodate the toddler.

"I overheard your name. You're new at the hospital, aren't you?" the woman said. "I'm Kate Franco and this is my daughter Tara. My husband, Tony, is the staff attorney."

"It's good to meet you." Jan was glad the woman had introduced herself. "There must be a lot of hospital employees with kids here."

"Quite a few," Kate agreed. "Oh, there's one of them now."

Following her gesture toward a third-grade classroom, Jan nearly forgot to breathe.

Near the doorway stood a man with tawny hair as thick as it had been seven years ago, while the September sunlight gave his skin a bronze glow. She had no time to prepare before intense green eyes, the same color as Kimmie's, fixed on her with a startled expression.

"That's Dr. Zack Sargent, one of the obstetricians," Kate noted. "Would you like me to introduce you?"

Swallowing a lump in her throat, Jan dredged up the words. "No, thanks. I'm sure I'll meet him at work."

What was he doing here? He and his wife—her name

was Rima, Jan had heard—hadn't been married long enough to have a third-grader. "Which kid is his?"

Nodding at a dark-skinned girl in jeans and an aqua T-shirt, Kate said, "That's his stepdaughter, Berry. Her mom died when she was five and he's been raising her alone."

"How…fatherly." Jan struggled to grasp what this meant. For years she'd carried an image of her former fiancé as a happily married man, but Zack was widowed. Yet he obviously had strong parental instincts.

What was that going to mean when he learned about their daughter? She'd assumed he would want as little to do with Kimmie now as he had when, early in Jan's pregnancy, he'd signed papers waiving his paternal rights.

When she glanced back toward him she saw Zack turn in her direction. Mercifully, the teacher in the doorway finished talking to another parent and reached to shake Zack's hand. While he was busy, Jan made an excuse to Kate and strode along the walkway as fast as her high-heeled pumps would carry her.

Her heart thumped, leaving her breathless. Even after all this time, her fingers remembered the softness of Zack's hair and the rough texture of his cheeks in the morning. She hadn't expected this deep-down yearning… Or this jolt of fear.

While he apparently hadn't seen her with Kimmie, he must be wondering why Jan was at the school. She'd omitted any mention of her daughter from her résumé or Facebook page, focusing strictly on business. She'd hoped to dodge him until she could select the right opportunity at work, but that possibility had flown out the window.

She was going to have to face her former fiancé sooner rather than later.

WHAT HAD JAN BEEN DOING at school this morning? As far as Zack knew, she'd never married and he'd heard nothing about children.

He speculated about her reasons as he prepped for surgery later that morning. Giving up a child for adoption might sound easy in the abstract, but Zack had seen patients suffer stress and self-blame years after relinquishing a baby. He'd experienced some of the same pangs himself. The fact that Rima was a single parent with a daughter had been part of the initial attraction, a way to atone at least partially for his mistakes.

And he'd made big ones.

It wouldn't surprise him if Jan had eventually adopted a child, perhaps a preschooler from a troubled home. *Which gives us even more in common than a shared passion for the egg-donor program.* And a painful past he'd like to put behind them.

Earlier, her stunned expression when their gazes met had reverberated through him. Regardless of the public setting, he'd nearly gone over to talk to her.

To apologize, again, more thoroughly than the brief conversation they'd had over the phone when he'd tracked her down months after their breakup, late in her pregnancy. It had taken Zack much too long to learn the truth about the allegations against her, which had led to their parting, and to realize how wrong he'd been. By then her anger toward him had hardened into an impenetrable wall. And he'd made commitments to someone else who needed him badly.

All the same, the sight of Jan today had punched him in the gut. He'd forgotten how vibrant she was. That rich dark hair, those teasing eyes…

Zack brought himself up sharply. They had to establish

a new relationship as fellow professionals, able to discuss medical issues without distractions.

"Is everything all right, Doctor?" Surgical nurse Stacy Raditch was already scrubbed in for the operation.

"First day of school," he said. "It's hard to see my little girl growing up."

"Berry's such a darling!" The young nurse always made a point of chatting with his daughter at staff events. "What grade is she in?"

"Third." Glad for the change of subject, Zack kept up a desultory conversation as they went into the operating room. He then spoke with the patient, who was undergoing a microsurgical procedure called a tubal anastomosis to reverse a tubal ligation that had rendered her sterile. After her previous marriage to a man who didn't want children, she and her new husband were eager to restore her fertility.

Using a surgical microscope and other specialized tools, Zack would reopen her fallopian tubes to allow fertilization. "As I told you, there's a high rate of success with this procedure," he assured the woman. "You may even be able to become pregnant naturally, without in vitro."

"That would be wonderful." Her hair hidden beneath a cap, she smiled up at him weakly. "Our insurance doesn't cover those high-tech infertility treatments, so…"

Zack touched her shoulder reassuringly. Her situation wasn't unusual. The miracles accomplished by modern technology came at a price. That was why he was pushing to establish a grant program for infertile patients. If he or one of the other obstetricians who agreed with him managed to win the hospital's promotional Hope Challenge, they'd have a $100,000 charitable donation to start their fund.

Only three months to go. The physician achieving the

highest pregnancy rate with infertile patients could choose where to donate the prize money. Zack was only in fourth place so far, in part because he devoted a lot of his time to learning new surgical and implantation techniques rather than scheduling additional patients. Of the three doctors ahead of him, only one—Dr. Paige Brennan—openly backed his plan.

He resolutely cleared all other considerations from his mind. He faced a delicate surgery requiring precision to reconnect tissues by stitching them together.

Right now, this patient was the only one that mattered.

JAN SPENT THE MORNING settling into her office on the hospital's ground floor and meeting some of the fertility-clinic staff. Originally, she'd planned to arrive months earlier, but she'd been held up by contractual obligations at her Houston job. Now she had to play catch-up.

She'd gotten in touch ahead of time with Melissa Everhart, who as coordinator for in vitro fertilization—IVF—would play a major role in working with the hospital's future roster of egg donors. Finally, today, they would meet face-to-face. Jan also was introduced to Dr. Cole Rattigan, the new head of the men's fertility program, who had the office next to hers, and Karen Wiggins, the financial counselor for infertile patients.

How ironic she'd become pregnant by accident, Jan reflected while eating a sandwich at her desk. Still, having a child gave her a powerful connection with the women and couples she served.

How was Kimmie faring at school? Was she making new friends? When Jan initially learned she was pregnant, she'd been eager to give up the baby and reclaim her life. Somewhere during the pregnancy, though, she'd ceased to be a separate person and had become part of a pair so interwoven she had a hard time thinking of herself without Kimmie.

Still, her daughter was growing up. Second grade already.

Jan turned her attention to preparing notes for tomorrow's organizational staff meeting. No two egg-donor programs were exactly alike. A lot of decisions had to be made before their official launch next spring.

The doctors would continue to rely on other egg banks until then. Luckily, there were quite a few in Southern California.

Jan's job was to establish an in-house donor program. In addition to soliciting and screening women as potential donors, she planned to implement a method called shared cycles that eased the financial burden for some patients while increasing the supply of available eggs. Sometimes a woman produced viable eggs but still needed to have them fertilized in the laboratory and then implanted, perhaps because of blocked fallopian tubes. If she chose to share her cycle, the patient donated half of her retrieved eggs—usually far more than could be safely implanted in her own womb—to another woman who couldn't produce any. The term *shared cycles* derived from the fact that both donor and recipient took hormones on the same schedule to prepare for simultaneous implantation. The recipient paid for the eggs, enough to cover a significant portion of the donor mom's expenses.

There were drawbacks, of course. The woman producing the eggs might prefer to have them frozen for her own use later. Plus, not everyone felt comfortable with the idea of someone else carrying and raising her genetic child, especially since there was no guarantee she herself would become pregnant. Still, for those short of money, it made dreams affordable.

A tap at her half-open door broke Jan's concentration. "Yes?"

A deep green gaze met hers. Sensitive mouth, questioning expression, powerful shoulders she'd clung to when they made love... Why did she have to remember that now?

"Zack." Her mouth was too dry to say more.

"Hi." He tilted his head invitingly. "Jan, we need to talk. I'm grabbing lunch in the cafeteria. Care to join me?"

No point in making excuses. "I could use a coffee." *And some divine intervention.*

With what she hoped passed for a smile, Jan got to her feet.

## Chapter Two

Now that he'd started the ball rolling, Zack wished he'd planned what to say. He'd stopped in to see Jan because he wanted to talk privately before tomorrow's meeting. As professionals, they needed to establish a good working relationship.

He also wanted to find out why she'd been at the school this morning.

In the cafeteria, Zack chose a sandwich plate with fruit while Jan poured herself a coffee. He paid for both orders and glanced around the busy dining room. Although there were a few free tables, his three years here had given Zack a healthy respect for the grapevine. Gossip spread rapidly, fed by certain nosy individuals. You never knew who might be listening.

"Let's try the patio," he said.

"Sure." Jan's expression betrayed nothing.

Eight years ago, when he'd met her at the hospital where they'd both worked in Los Angeles, she'd been an open-faced twenty-two-year-old with a newly minted nursing degree and a joyful aura he'd warmed to instantly.

Now her long lashes hid her gaze and she kept her full lips clamped shut. Well, what had he expected?

Outside, Zack was relieved to see the patio empty. Surrounded by a flowering hedge and a few squatty palm trees, its handful of tables offered privacy.

He set his tray on one. "I suppose you've heard we'll be working together."

Coffee sloshed onto the table. "What do you mean?"

Although there was no official designation, Zack had assumed Dr. Tartikoff would tell her of his interest. "I'm eager to help get the egg-donor program off the ground," he said, mopping her spilled coffee with a paper napkin. "I've been learning new techniques from Dr. T and brushing up on my embryology with Alec Denny's help. You'll need a physician to work with you closely. I've arranged my schedule so I'll be available."

Still on her feet, she glared at him. "Why are you doing this?"

Zack could see he'd gone about this the wrong way. "I was excited about the project before I had any idea who the director would be. Please, sit down. Unless there's coffee on your chair."

Jan ran her hand over the seat. "All clear." She edged onto it as if ready to bolt. Collar-length hair fell forward, shielding her face. A man didn't have to be psychic to read that body language.

"I came to Safe Harbor to be part of something cutting-edge. When I heard Dr. Tartikoff had been hired, I was over the moon." Helping women and couples have babies had become a passion for Zack, perhaps because he'd had to give up his own child all those years ago.

*Don't mention that. She's tense enough already.*

Jan released a long breath. "You'll be at tomorrow's meeting? Dr. T hasn't sent me a complete list of who he invited. He doesn't seem as organized as he used to be."

"I guess you know he got married and has young

twins," Zack said. "He may be a powerhouse, but those late nights take their toll."

"Does he run roughshod over his wife? I understand she's a nurse."

Obviously, Jan hadn't met Bailey. Still, Zack understood the question. He'd heard the brilliant but abrasive Dr. T had terrified his staff in Boston even while inspiring them. "She's as tough as he is, in her own charming way."

"Glad to hear it."

Zack took a moment to eat while weighing his next move. They'd broken the ice, so he'd accomplished that much. Despite the curiosity nagging at him, he'd better stay on neutral ground for now.

"You've heard about the Hope Challenge?" She couldn't participate, since she wasn't a doctor, but the results might affect her program.

"Owen's been raving about it." She'd relaxed enough to refer to Dr. T by his first name. A good sign. "I gather there's been positive feedback in blogs and from the press. I presume the point is to promote the hospital and the fertility program."

"It helps establish our name recognition with the public," Zack agreed. "Not that we're short of patients."

"This contest—how does it work?" She, too, was sticking to neutral topics, thank goodness. "Does it count conceptions, live births or total number of babies born?"

"Confirmed conceptions," Zack said. "Each pregnancy counts once, no matter how many babies a woman is carrying. We don't want to encourage multiple births." Those were dangerous, as Zack frequently explained to his patients. Having triplets or quads might sound like heaven when a couple had been struggling to achieve a pregnancy, but the results could be devastating if the babies were premature or had birth defects.

"There's a hundred-thousand-dollar prize for this contest, right?" Jan said. "That's very generous of the hospital corporation."

"The winning doctor gets to designate the charity. I'm pushing for whoever wins to establish a grant program for fertility patients."

"That's a great idea!" Jan's face lit with interest. "How would you choose the recipients? Strictly by financial need?"

Zack had given this a lot of thought. "I'd like us to consider the woman's age as well, and whether she already has children. If this is her only chance, that would weigh on her side. We might also look at her medical and psychological history, although I'd hate to be in the position of passing judgment."

"Still, having a program in place would help at least *some* patients." Jan frowned. "Isn't there a competing proposal? Something to do with a counseling center?"

"You've met our administrator, Dr. Mark Rayburn?" Seeing her nod, Zack continued. "His wife, pediatrician Samantha Forrest, set up an informal program a few years ago to offer peer counseling. The idea was to reach families, teen moms and others who might shy away from a formal environment with a lot of paperwork. It's done some good, thanks to volunteers, but it's never established an endowment and always seems to be on the verge of failing. The last I heard, it may lose its quarters at the city's community center."

"Well-intentioned," Jan murmured. "Not likely to become self-sustaining, if it hasn't done so already. I like your idea better."

He felt a glimmer of their old connection. What a pleasure it had been, after growing up with cold, critical parents, to bat ideas back and forth freely with Jan.

Things had been different with Rima. Her health issues and Berry's care had dominated their relationship, as Zack had expected from the start.

His thoughts returned to Jan. While he could play it safe and leave the conversation on a high note, eventually they'd have to discuss the elephant in the room. Might as well do that now.

He decided to edge into the subject. "In case you're looking for an after-school sitter, did Kate Franco mention that her sister Mary Beth Ellroy runs a home day care center? They pick up my daughter Berry at school, and usually they're willing to let her sleep over when I'm on call."

He'd employed two nannies when Berry was younger. Although they'd both worked well for a while, parting had been an emotional wrench. Also, Zack had slipped into a routine of relying on the nannies when he should have been clearing as much time as possible for his daughter. Since Berry had started school, he'd relied on Mary Beth, who offered a home environment that included her own three children.

"Kate didn't say anything." Jan fiddled with her empty cup.

"I'm not prying." Oh, the hell he wasn't. "Yes, I am. I saw you at school today. You have a child there?"

"My mother lives fifteen minutes away."

What did that have to do with anything? Oh, right, day care. "She watches your—is it a son or daughter?"

She leaned back, eyes averted. "Daughter."

Eight years ago she'd been pregnant with a girl. His daughter. A speck of suspicion he'd been unwilling to acknowledge swelled in his gut. "I hadn't heard that you'd married. I thought maybe you'd adopted."

"Adopted?"

For heaven's sake, enough beating around the bush. "What's going on, Jan?"

Deep breath. Long pause.

*This can't be what I think it is.* All these years, Zack had imagined his daughter adopted by a married couple. He'd worried whether he'd done the right thing by waiving his rights and tried to convince himself he had. Jan hadn't mentioned any particular family or adoption center when she thrust the relinquishment papers in front of him, and matters had been so tense he hadn't pressed her. Still, it had never occurred to him she might betray his trust completely.

In fairness, by the time he'd learned she'd been wrongly accused of harming a patient, and realized how badly he'd let her down, he'd been engaged to Rima. When Jan brushed off his apology and insisted her family was helping her through the pregnancy, Zack had rationalized away his uneasiness and left matters in her hands.

Now he waited apprehensively for her explanation.

"Well," Jan began. Just then the patio door opened and two nurses came out.

Zack struggled to hide his annoyance. One of the nurses was Stacy, who eyed them wearing a troubled expression. She'd made no secret of liking Zack, although he'd never given her any reason to think he returned her interest. While she seemed both pleasant and skilled as a scrub nurse, he'd never felt so much as a quiver of excitement around her.

The other woman, Erica Vaughn, assisted Dr. T in surgery. She'd moved here from Boston a little over a year ago to join his team, at his request. As she swooped toward them, Zack remembered with chagrin that she and Jan must be old acquaintances.

"Jan! It's great to see you." Erica paused, lunch tray in hand. "Are we interrupting?"

"We were…" Jan broke off, registering the nurse's enlarged abdomen. "You're pregnant!"

Taking that as an invitation, Erica joined them at the table. Stacy did the same. "I got married. Something about this town seems to foster romance. I never expected it to happen to me, but here we are. I'm seven months along."

As Zack tried to pretend an interest in the discussion, his thoughts kept returning to the question of Jan's daughter. Had Jan really kept their child and denied him contact all these years?

He'd been angry at himself for betraying her trust. Now, it seemed, she might have betrayed his, and unlike him, she'd had full knowledge of what she was doing. Although he'd been quick to judge and arrogant in his refusal to listen to her side of the story, he hadn't deliberately done her an injustice. Was this her idea of punishment?

A cell phone rang. Everyone instinctively reached for pocket or purse.

It was Jan's. She listened, a worried expression crossing her face. "You're sure she isn't seriously hurt, Mrs. Humphreys? You must be concerned or you wouldn't have called."

Zack felt a snap of alarm. The second-grade teacher didn't panic easily. When Mrs. Humphreys taught Berry last year, he'd admired her ability to stay calm.

"Yes, that sounds like her…. Oh, dear. I'd better come by. My mother will be picking her up, but she can't deal with this. Thank you for telling me."

After she clicked off, Erica said, "What's happened to Kimmie?"

*Kimmie.* So that was Jan's daughter's name. His daughter, too?

Erica had obviously known the girl when Jan worked with Dr. T in Boston. Zack's chest grew tight at the realization that, if this was his child, other people here at the hospital had watched her grow during the toddler years, while he'd remained ignorant. The thought burned inside him.

Grabbing her purse, Jan stood up. "On the playground she rescued a stray kitten from some dogs. That's my little girl. She can't stand to see an animal suffer."

"Is she okay?" Zack demanded, more forcefully than he'd intended. Stacy frowned, clearly puzzled.

"A few scratches. The school nurse is cleaning and bandaging them." Jan shook her head. "Kimmie won't let go of the kitten. It's clinging to her and she insists on keeping it."

"Poor little thing." Erica might have meant either the child or the kitten, or both.

"I'll let the secretary know I have to run out. Thank goodness my staff meeting isn't till tomorrow. Bye, everybody."

Zack snatched his tray and took off in her wake. Never mind the questions on the nurses' faces. If this was his daughter…

Damn. He had to find out before it drove him crazy.

In the cafeteria he set the tray on a conveyor belt and followed Jan, attempting to keep his manner casual. None of the other diners appeared to take special notice.

Jan was headed for her office. Lingering nearby, Zack checked the schedule in his phone. A surgery had been canceled after the patient suffered an allergy attack, freeing up the next two hours. He had office patients scheduled beginning at four o'clock.

When Jan emerged he fell into step beside her. "I'll come with you."

"Why?" she demanded. "There's no reason for you to be there."

"Isn't there?"

She pushed open the side exit. "We can continue this discussion later."

"Jan…" On the sidewalk, he paused to let a couple of workmen pass, trundling dollies piled with crates. The hospital hadn't quite finished remodeling its basement laboratories for the fertility program.

Jan swung toward him, eyes brimming with worry. "You're a parent. You should understand. It's Kimmie's first day at a new school and she's upset. Plus, she's stubborn. If she's glommed on to that kitten, she'll turn the whole place upside down rather than let go."

"I'd like to understand. I have the disadvantage of not knowing her personally." Zack hadn't meant to be sarcastic. Under stress he instinctively used the tone his father had during his childhood.

She folded her arms. "I knew you'd react like this."

"Excuse me?"

Instead of responding, Jan swung away and hurried along the sidewalk toward a row of spaces reserved for department heads. "Zack, this isn't the time or place… Oh, damn!"

A double-parked panel truck was blocking several cars. One of them must be hers.

"They went that-a-way." He indicated the path the workmen had taken. They'd disappeared around a corner. "The freight elevator's back there." Before she could figure out the men probably hadn't had time to summon the elevator, he added, "We can take my car."

"Don't you have patients?" she protested.

"Right now I have more patience than you do." The weak attempt at humor beat responding with further sarcasm. "To answer your question, I had a surgery cancel. Come on, Jan. Let's talk in the car."

Her dark eyes pierced him. Yet he didn't miss the quirk of her mouth that hinted she might be yielding. "Well…"

Zack took her arm. "Watch where you step. Those trucks are rough on the pavement." He guided her around a dip in the surface where he'd nearly tripped that morning.

He expected resistance. Instead, as they walked toward the parking structure, Jan's shoulders sagged. "I've been dreading this."

"Your daughter getting into trouble?" All he could see was the top of her head, the brown hair parted slightly off center. He'd forgotten how short she was, perhaps because she had such an oversize personality. "She must be a little firecracker."

"I meant I've been dreading talking to you."

A delivery truck rumbled past. "Is that because…" He hated shouting over the noise. Besides, there was no sense broadcasting their personal issues to anyone nearby. "To be continued when we're in the car."

"I hope Kimmie's not freaking out. Moving from a house to a small apartment, being separated from her friends—it's been hard on her." Worry sped her pace.

Zack felt a spark of protectiveness. But he wasn't sure who it was directed toward, Jan or the little girl.

Reaching his blue hybrid van on the lower level, he used the remote control to open the locks. As Jan jumped into the passenger seat, he slid behind the wheel. With the doors finally shielding them, he couldn't hold back his painfully important question. "Is Kimmie my daughter?"

Jan gripped the armrest and gave him the answer he'd been both wishing for and fearing. "Yes, she is."

In that moment, Zack understood his world would never be the same again.

## Chapter Three

When Zack's knuckles whitened over the steering wheel,
Jan saw how badly she'd hurt him. But she couldn't deal
with this now, when she was so worried about Kimmie.
Even a hint something might be wrong with her daughter
threatened to shake her world.

"You promised to drive, so drive!" she snapped.

Jaw clamped so tight she could almost hear his teeth
grinding, Zack backed out and headed toward the street.
Jan braced for more questions, but he seemed caught up in
navigating through hospital traffic and across congested
Safe Harbor Boulevard.

"She loves animals." It felt better to talk than to sit in
silence. "That's her passion. In Houston, we fostered kittens for a shelter until people adopted them."

"I see." His eyes hardened into emeralds.

"By the time I decided to keep her you were engaged
to someone else," Jan said tautly. "I was hurt and angry,
and figured it would just make more trouble for you."

"All these years…"

"I can't undo the past."

"That's no excuse." He tapped the brake at a stop sign
before shooting forward.

"What would you have done?" she challenged. "Would
you have dropped your fiancée and come running to be

a full-time daddy? Or kept me dangling on a hook with legal maneuvers, stuck in Southern California when I was offered a great job in Boston?"

"That isn't the point." He still didn't meet her gaze.

"I was barely hanging on to my sanity and my career, thanks to… Oh, never mind. Let's not fight." They were approaching the school, anyway.

A little of the tension seeped out of him. "You're right about one thing. Beating each other up emotionally won't undo the past."

"I'm glad we agree on that." Jan braced for what lay ahead. In the next few minutes, she had to soothe Kimmie, decide what to do about the kitten and prevent the issues between her and Zack from spilling over in public.

What was going to happen when he recovered from the initial shock? He already had a daughter who depended on him, and he and Jan had to work together at the hospital. If only he were willing to keep this whole matter under wraps…

Except Kimmie kept pestering her for a daddy. And whether Jan liked it or not, Zack appeared more than ready to fill that role.

HARD TO BELIEVE he'd driven almost this same route a few hours ago with no idea of the jolt that lay ahead, Zack thought. Berry had been eager to see her old friends, missing them keenly even though he'd arranged visits with her best friend Cindy during the summer. Berry had also attended a day-camp program that took her to museums and theme parks. But going to school meant returning to home ground.

Now that same school loomed like alien territory. Zack was about to meet a daughter he'd believed out of reach and unknowable.

The prospect excited him. It was also intimidating. What was she like, this precious little girl? How would she feel about him?

He'd known of her existence—in the abstract—for seven years. As for Kimmie… "What did you tell her about her father?" he asked as they reached the school.

"That he lived far away and had another family." Jan clasped her hands together. "Recently she's started asking questions. I've been changing the subject a lot."

"You couldn't seriously expect to keep the truth from her forever." He found a parking spot easily. In another half hour, parents would pour in to pick up their kids.

"I've been forced to live in the moment. Making ends meet, putting out fires. Raising a child by myself, I couldn't see beyond the next few months."

"In other words, you figured you'd deal with a serious issue like Kimmie's paternity by the seat of your pants."

"That's right."

She'd always been impulsive, relying more on instinct than reason. Years ago, he hadn't minded their differences. He'd found her a refreshing change from his parents' rigid perfectionism.

Together, they exited the car. "Visitors are supposed to sign in at the office," Zack mentioned.

"We can skip that. The campus will be teeming with parents in a few minutes." She set off at a rapid clip, clearly anxious to reach the classroom.

Zack supposed it didn't hurt to break a rule once in a while, especially since the teacher was expecting them. Well, expecting Jan. He'd have to be careful what he said. He didn't want to break the news of his identity to Kimmie in front of others.

They hurried along the walkway between classroom wings. The babble of children's voices floated from a room to their left. On the right, Zack heard a teacher reading aloud, animating the story with different voices. He enjoyed doing that, too. It had been a letdown when Berry began reading books on her own, without daddy's help. Of course, he was proud of her, too.

How was Berry going to react to this news? He'd never mentioned the daughter he gave up for adoption.

Concerned she might fear Zack would abandon her, too, he and Rima had agreed there was no point raising the topic until Berry was older. It had been tricky enough explaining her birth father's death in a motorcycle accident, glossing over his struggle with alcohol. Another topic left for a later date.

Jan wasn't the only person who postponed dealing with difficult subjects, Zack conceded.

Outside Mrs. Humphreys's classroom, her pace slowed. "Do you suppose they took the kitty inside?"

"The teacher sometimes brings her pet chinchilla to class, so having an animal around isn't unusual," he recalled. "She might be treating this as a nature lesson."

Jan tapped at the door. Mrs. Humphreys's round, pleasant face glanced out a louvered window before she admitted them.

"I'm sorry for disrupting your class," Jan said.

"This is a good opportunity to make the students aware of the problems of overpopulation among cats and dogs." The teacher ushered them inside. "Dr. Sargent?"

"Ms. Garcia's car was blocked, so I offered to drive her. We work together," he explained.

A roomful of young faces peered at them curiously. Zack had no trouble picking out Kimmie. While the other kids sat around low tables, his daughter stood near the front, an orange-striped kitten clinging to her shoulder. Dark hair like Jan's tumbled down to her rumpled pink blouse. Adhesive bandage strips sprouted along her arms and knees beneath a frilly skirt. Her mother ought to dress her in jeans and T-shirts as he did Berry, Zack thought. It was much more practical.

A pair of vivid green eyes swept past him and fixed on Jan. That elfin face with its pointed chin was almost a mirror of her mom's.

Zack's heart turned over. *My daughter.* Seven years ago, aching over the loss of trust in the woman he loved, he'd given Kimmie up in the belief it was the best thing for everyone. Here stood the proof he'd been wrong.

"I'm naming her Smidge," Kimmie announced. "See how tiny she is?"

Jan's mouth twisted. "She's adorable, but our lease doesn't allow pets."

"Mom!"

Mrs. Humphreys intervened smoothly. "If my husband didn't have allergies, I'd take her. I'll tell you what. I've got a pet carrier in my car I keep in case I spot a stray. You can borrow if you don't mind scrubbing it carefully before returning it."

"I'm afraid that doesn't solve the main problem," Jan responded.

Rummaging in a drawer, the teacher produced a frayed business card. "This is for the Oahu Lane Shelter. It's a small no-kill facility less than a mile north of the hospital. Ilsa Ivy is the driving force behind it. Just mention that I sent you."

While Zack wasn't keen on having a cat in his car, even in a carrier, he felt sorry for the little thing. Moreover, he didn't want his first interaction with Kimmie to put him in a bad light. "We could drop it off on the way back to work."

The little girl glowered as if he'd suggested doing violence to the creature. "I'm keeping her!"

"No, you aren't." Jan studied the card. "They're closed on Mondays. Surely they have someone there to care for the animals?"

"I think a volunteer stops by in the morning," Mrs. Humphreys said. "Could you keep it overnight?"

"Please!" Kimmie begged, quivering with longing. Zack suspected she'd have dropped to her knees and clasped her hands in a melodramatic gesture had she not been holding the kitten.

"The landlord lives upstairs from us," Jan said unhappily. "He was very firm on the subject. If we violate the lease, we'll have to leave."

Standoff. Zack saw a solution, even if he didn't like it.

He'd never cared for having animals in the home. As a doctor, he'd observed the problems that could arise, from allergies and infected scratches to rare, serious disease transmission, sometimes resulting in birth defects. Of course, he recognized the work done by service dogs and the emotional value of animal companions. In his house, however, he maintained a strict no-pets policy.

Keeping a kitten overnight didn't exactly violate that policy, though. Without time to think further, he said, "I suppose it wouldn't hurt to keep it at my place. There's a downstairs bathroom that should be safe enough."

Jan looked grateful. "We can pick up cat food and a litter box on the way."

"Who's he?" Kimmie demanded, staring at Zack. Obviously she wasn't about to relinquish her kitty to just anyone.

"This is Dr. Zachary Sargent, an old friend of mine." To him, Jan added, "Zack, this is my daughter, Kimmie."

He considered squatting to reach her level, but that

seemed awkward. Instead, he simply added, "Call me
Zack. I have a daughter in the third grade named Berry.
I'm sure she'll be delighted to play with the cat this eve-
ning."

"I'll get the carrier. Keep an eye on the class, please."
Seizing the moment, Mrs. Humphreys went out.

Left alone with the children, Zack tried to figure out
what to say. *What's your favorite subject?* struck him
as lame. He was about to ask what their favorite books
were when Jan leaped into the gap. "How many of you
kids have pets?"

About half the hands went up. "Do turtles count?" one
little girl asked.

"You bet."

A boy hoisted his stuffed eagle. "What about Natty?"

Kimmie wrinkled her nose. "You can't count stuffed
animals. They aren't real."

"Who says?"

Around the room, the kids began debating among
themselves. Raised hands turned into gesturing hands.
Stuffed animals squeaked angrily.

How did an adult intervene in a dispute like this? Zack
wondered. Berry had never been argumentative. When
Rima described her as a compliant child, he hadn't understood what that meant. He was beginning to get the
picture.

"They seem like people," a blond boy announced, his
voice rising above the rest as he wielded a fuzzy green
brontosaurus. Zack recognized him as Brady Franco, Kate
and Tony's son. "There aren't any more dinosaurs, so
Sneezer isn't real. He still has feelings."

Zack recalled how Berry clung to her lion, Roar, whenever she was upset. "We invest emotions in our stuffed

animals," he said. "So to us, they take on real character-
istics."

The children stopped talking. Some frowned, while
others stared at him blankly. Apparently *invest* and *char-
acteristics* weren't second-grade vocabulary words.

"Good point, Dr. Sargent," Jan said tactfully. "Oh,
here's Mrs. Humphreys!" Relief showed in her face.

Zack shared the feeling.

JAN GAZED WISTFULLY at the two-story blue house with a
picket fence, a rose trellis and white shutters. If it had appeared in a real-estate ad, she'd have clipped it, if only
to dream about.

"Renting?" she asked as Zack stopped in the driveway.

"Bought it three years ago. The mortgage makes for
a tight budget, but I wanted a secure place for Berry to
grow up." He glanced into the backseat, where the kitten
was mewing pitifully in its carrier. "She's had a lot of loss
and upheaval in her life."

"What happened to her birth father?" Jan asked as
she got out.

"Motorcycle accident." Zack didn't explain further.

They'd stopped at a store to pick up supplies, Zack
waiting in the car while Jan ran inside. "Shall I drop by
in the morning to pick up the kitten?" she asked as she removed the ventilated plastic carton and toted it toward the
porch. Inside, Smidge scrabbled about to keep her balance.

"According to the card, the animal center doesn't open
till nine. I'll swing by at lunch tomorrow and take her
over." Zack spoke briskly as he let them inside.

Stepping into the entryway, Jan caught the scent of
lemon cleanser. The tile floor gleamed, and in the living
room to her right, the carpet showed only a few traces of
footprints on the vacuumed surface. Beige draperies set

off a red couch, splashy yellow, red and white throw cushions, and a couple of zebra-striped armchairs.

Among a tabletop of framed photos, a beaming image
stood out: a smiling young woman with cocoa-colored
skin, her wiry hair gathered into a topknot with stray
curls rioting around her face.

"Did your wife choose the furniture?" Jan guessed.
"It's very cheerful."

"Yes, for our apartment in L.A." Zack crossed the hallway and opened a door to reveal a bathroom beneath a
bend in the staircase. "I took the job at Safe Harbor a few
months after she died. Berry and I needed a fresh start,
and this was a good environment for her."

Much as she admired his devotion to his stepdaughter, Jan couldn't ignore a twist of envy. He'd fallen for
another woman very quickly after their breakup. She'd
told herself it had been on the rebound, but his defection
hurt. Also, by the time he married, he'd known Jan was
pregnant, yet he'd willingly given up both Jan and their
child for a new love and her little girl.

*Stop thinking about that. You have important arrange-
ments to make.* For Kimmie's sake and Berry's, they had
to agree on how to proceed.

First things first. Gazing around, Jan saw this was
merely a powder room. They'd have to wedge the litter
box next to the toilet and set the water bowl as far away as
possible. The dish of kitten food could go under the edge
of the cabinet, which left scarcely any room on the floor.

"Do you have a big towel?" she asked. "Smidge
shouldn't have to lie on the hard tile."

"Sure." Zack reached past her to a shelf piled with
towels. His nearness made her keenly aware of the way
his dark red open-collared shirt fit the strong contours

of his body. As he brushed past, Jan caught the scent of his light aftershave.

Inside the carrier, the kitten mewed sorrowfully. "It's okay, Smidge," she murmured. "We'll get you settled in a minute."

Zack lifted down a fluffy yellow towel edged with lace. "If you refer to it by name, you'll get attached."

Disturbed by his coldness, Jan nearly changed her mind and insisted on taking the kitten home. Then she remembered the landlord's finger stabbing at the no-pets section of their lease as if the fate of the earth hung in the balance if she broke it. "Don't you have a ratty old towel? She could ruin this one."

"Good idea." He refolded the towel, thrust it back on the shelf and disappeared into a hallway. A moment later, from deep in the house, she heard a door open, presumably to the garage.

Setting the carrier on the floor, Jan tried to coax the kitten out. Its little eyes peered up at her fearfully. "What happened to you?" she asked in the indulgent tone reserved for babies and small animals. "Where's your mommy?" She had enough experience with kittens to know this one was old enough to be weaned, so perhaps it had gone hunting and gotten lost.

Smidge stopped cringing and ventured a paw out. A moment later it was sniffing Jan's leg. She patted the soft fur. "What a cutie."

Zack had been right. She was close to losing her heart. Who could resist this little creature? she wondered as she picked it up.

Zack, for one. Her landlord, for another.

Strong footsteps approached. "How's this?" Edging past her, Zack laid a tattered pink towel on the floor. Judging by the color it must have been red before surviving a zillion washings. Still, it looked thick and comfortable.

As she held Smidge in the doorway, he opened the package of kitty litter and poured some carefully into the box, then filled the water and food bowls. "She should be okay now, right? Should I pour her some milk?"

"It might go bad. You can warm some when you get home."

The room lacked a window. Still, cats could see in the dark, and the door was high enough off the floor to let in air. Although tempted to suggest they provide some toys or, better yet, choose a larger bathroom, Jan figured she'd be pushing her luck.

It was after three o'clock. In just a few hours, Zack would return from work and, as he'd said, Berry would most likely make a beeline for the kitten.

Jan released Smidge onto the towel. "Time to go," Zack said from behind her.

"Bye, little one. You'll be fine." Hoping it was true, she drew back and let Zack close the door. Her breath caught as a plaintive meow followed them.

"Kittens sound a lot like human babies," Zack observed. "I've read that's why people respond to them so strongly."

*Also, they have hearts.* Best not to insult him. "We should go."

"You can wash your hands in the kitchen."

"Right. Thanks." At his direction, Jan went past a home office, which she saw at a glance was furnished with a sturdy wooden desk and swivel chair, computer and bookcase. In the back of the house, they crossed a family room filled with a couch, upholstered chairs and a large TV. Through a sliding glass door, she noted a patio, fenced yard and gingerbread-style playhouse. "I'll bet Berry adores that."

"The playhouse? She only uses it when her friend Cindy comes over." He indicated the sink in the spacious kitchen that opened off the family room. "You can freshen up in here."

State-of-the-art refrigerator, oven and stove top. Burnished cabinets and a breakfast nook. *If only Kimmie could grow up in a place like this.*

Jan squelched the thought. The only way her daughter could live in such a cozy house was if she came to stay with her father. And that was a possibility Jan refused to consider.

Hands washed and dried, she turned and nearly ran into Zack. "Before we go," he said, "we should talk."

Jan didn't ask about what. Her throat was too dry to let a word escape. Besides, she already knew the answer.

No more avoidance. Whatever the next step was, they were about to take it.

# Chapter Four

Eight years ago Zack's life had turned upside down without warning. Now it was happening again. In one day, he'd learned his daughter hadn't been given to strangers but was growing up with her mother...and that he could and *would* have a relationship with Kimmie. Not in the distant future, but right now.

So he sat across the table from the woman he'd once loved, trying to figure out how to make up for lost time with his daughter and how to deal with a raging storm of anger, disappointment and guilt.

An image of Kimmie standing in front of the class remained etched in his mind. Dark hair falling around her intense face, chin lifted defiantly, she'd been ready to take on all comers.

She reminded him of Jan, back when the hospital in L.A. had accused her of harming a patient through ignorance and carelessness. At the time, Zack had seen Jan as stubbornly defending her wrongful actions.

She'd administered an overdose of medication, precipitating an attack that nearly cost an elderly man his life. The fact that he'd recovered had been a blessing, and enabled them to keep legal authorities out of it. Still, nothing changed the fact the man had been subjected to unnecessary harm, and the hospital had had to settle out of court with his family.

Zack had urged Jan to admit responsibility and drop her fight against being fired. Although he realized this black mark might end her career, he'd believed a person with integrity admitted his or her mistakes. While her inexperience might explain the error, it didn't excuse her obstinacy.

She'd furiously told him he ought to trust her, that the fault lay with the cardiologist and the nursing supervisor. She'd insisted the hospital had tampered with its records and conspired against her.

He'd considered her claims absurd. The doctor was a top specialist with an international reputation. As for the idea that the well-respected nursing supervisor would conspire to alter records—it didn't bear discussing.

After an argument, she'd thrown the engagement ring at him. A month later, when she informed him she was pregnant and intended to put the baby up for adoption, waiving his paternal rights had seemed a sensible solution for both them and the baby.

After that, events had moved swiftly in directions he couldn't have foreseen. Although Zack had wondered about his daughter, within months he'd committed himself to another woman and her child who needed him more.

Now he had to deal with the consequences. Angry as he might be about Jan's keeping him in the dark, he couldn't lay all the blame on her.

A lot depended on this discussion. With that temper of hers, she might abruptly decide to take Kimmie and leave the area. Zack didn't know what he'd do if that happened.

He folded his hands on the kitchen table. Best to start in a civil fashion. "Would you like something to drink?"

"Is this the last meal of an accused prisoner?" Jan angled her chair away from him defensively.

Zack ignored the sarcasm. "Orange juice, milk, ginger ale?"

"Orange juice, please."

He poured glasses for them both and returned. "We need to set ground rules."

"Such as?"

The first one was tough but important. "No blaming each other in front of people. That can only deteriorate into open hostility."

She took a sip before speaking. "Agreed."

"Also, we keep our personal business private. No discussing it at work."

Jan considered this. Studying her at close range, Zack noted her cheeks had lost some of their roundness, and her face had gained strength and maturity. Perhaps he didn't know her, or her temper, as well as he once had.

"People will find out we have a daughter together," she countered.

Zack recognized the news would inevitably spread. "I did mention to a few people that we were once engaged." Conversations in the operating room tended to cover a wide range of subjects, some quite personal.

"Which people?"

He tried to recall. "Dr. Paige Brennan. Stacy Raditch. The anesthesiologist. The circulating nurse." Operating rooms were busy places.

Jan's hands gripped the glass. Hanging on to her anger? "Still, we don't have to say anything more for the moment."

Good. They were on the same page so far. Now came the most sensitive part. "And I want time together. Just her and me."

Thank goodness she'd set down the glass or it might have cracked. Still, despite the tension in her muscles, she kept her tone level. "Before that can happen I have to break the news to her."

He should be the one to do that. Then Zack remembered the suspicious glare Kimmie had leveled at him in the classroom. To her, he was a stranger. Walking into Kimmie's life and declaring himself her father might suit his fantasies, but there was no telling how she'd react. Also, he needed to explain the situation to Berry, as well. "All right."

Jan's shoulders relaxed a little. "Now, how are we going to explain what happened without blame?"

"We can say we just…" Zack stopped. Just what? "I don't want Kimmie to think I didn't care what happened to her." He'd expected Jan to choose a loving, stable home for their little girl. An ideal home—as if such a thing existed.

"And I don't want her to get the impression I denied her a father all these years in order to punish you," Jan retorted.

*Even if it's true?* Avoiding blame was hard, Zack reflected. "We should coordinate our stories."

They hashed it out for a few minutes. The broken engagement was unavoidable. The hurt feelings and misunderstandings. But how to address the painful facts that Jan had left the area without telling him she'd kept Kimmie, and he'd married someone else and invested his love in another little girl?

"I don't see how we can soft-pedal this," Zack said.

An enigmatic smile lit Jan's face. "How about admitting we both screwed up?"

"That's the truth," he conceded. "I suppose it has the merit of being easy to remember."

"And avoids a sense of deception when the kids eventually find out whatever we try to hide. Which they will," she added.

"I hope they can forgive us," Zack said. "They're awfully young to understand how confused we were." He'd always seen his parents as towering figures, powerful and in control. No doubt his daughters would regard him the same way.

"Can't help that." Jan sighed. Except for the thinness in her cheeks, she hadn't changed much, he noted, as sunlight through the window highlighted her brown eyes and full mouth. "When are we going to do this?"

Much as he wanted to rush the process, Zack recognized the need for a few days to deal with their daughters' reactions. "I'd like to take Kimmie to lunch on Sunday."

"Shouldn't both of us spend time with her first... together?"

"She'll sense the tension." With an effort, Zack held on to his patience. "If we get testy with each other, that'll send the wrong message." This "date" was likely to set the tone for his and Kimmie's relationship, at least for the near future.

Jan gave a reluctant nod. "Next Sunday, you said?"

"Berry's in a choral group at church that's scheduled to sing at a convalescent home after services. I won't be picking her up until two." He'd mentally worked out the logistics. "That leaves plenty of time for lunch."

"Okay," Jan agreed, although she didn't look pleased. "I'll bring it up tonight."

"So will I." In an odd way, this was like a divorce, Zack thought. Although estranged, as parents he and Jan had to work together for the children's sake. He dug into his wallet for a card. "Here's my cell number. So we don't have to discuss the details at work."

"You think we can avoid it?"

"We can try."

She handed him a card from her purse. "Nice to meet you, Dr. Sargent."

"Same here, Nurse Garcia."

They'd reached a truce. Zack hoped it would hold.

"THAT MAN WHO TOOK Smidge?" Over the remains of dinner, Kimmie stared at Jan in disbelief. "He's my daddy?"

Jan dug her fork into her salad. After she'd picked up her daughter at Grandma Maria's house, happy chatter about school and the adventures of Mischief the bear had alternated with questions about Smidge. At home, Kimmie had cut up tomatoes and added them to the precut lettuce, standing on tiptoe at the counter while Jan deboned the roasted chicken she'd bought.

While they ate, Jan had sketched out the story of Zack and the broken engagement. Now here they sat at the table while her daughter struggled with the news.

"As I told you, I hadn't seen him since before you were born." Jan supposed she might have to repeat this story several times before the details make sense to Kimmie. "But now that we've moved back to California, it turns out we're going to be working together."

"He can't be my dad," Kimmie insisted. "He's that other girl's daddy. The one in the third grade."

"She's his stepdaughter."

"Why didn't he come visit me?" The plaintive note in her voice cut into Jan. *It's mostly my fault.*

"I told you your father lived far away and had another family." Thank goodness she had provided that much of the truth.

"I thought you meant in a galaxy far, far away," her daughter said. "Or in a castle. Or…something." From the dining nook, Kimmie stared across the front room.

Jan wished she could crawl into her daughter's mind to help sort things out. But she had to sit here and let Kimmie work through her own thoughts.

As she waited for whatever her daughter might say next, she noticed how cramped this room was compared to the house they'd rented in Houston. As for the worn couch, chairs and tables purchased at secondhand stores, they'd gained even more nicks and scrapes in the cross-country move. The lace doilies and ruffled pillows Jan had added to freshen them had taken a beating, as well. She made a mental note to replace them.

In a corner sat their small, outdated TV. Jan tried not to compare it to Zack's flat-screen TV or contrast these tight quarters with his house. Her salary at Safe Harbor would enable her to pay off the last of her student loans soon and start saving for a house. Meanwhile, she and Kimmie had a safe, comfortable place to live. Plenty of people in the world would be grateful for that.

"How come he loves that other little girl and he doesn't love me?" her daughter asked.

That hurt. "He doesn't know you because we've been living across the country, but he wants to. He's invited you to lunch on Sunday. Just you and him."

Kimmie's eyes widened as if a new thought had struck her. "I don't have to go live with him, do I?"

"Of course not!" Jan reached over to pat her arm. "You're still my little girl. Why do you ask that?"

"My friend Allie has to spend weekends with her daddy." Allie was her best friend in Texas.

"You don't have to do anything you don't want to," Jan promised. "I know this is a shock, but you *have* been wanting a daddy, and now he's here. I couldn't tell you about him until I'd spoken with him."

"That other girl…" Kimmie frowned, thinking so

hard Jan could almost feel the brain waves. "Where's her mommy?"

"She died." Jan hadn't asked the circumstances. Nor, she admitted with a twinge of guilt, had she considered how terrible his wife's death must have been for Zack. *I used to resent her. Now I wish she was alive.*

"What if I hate him?" Kimmie persisted. "Can I pick another daddy?"

Jan nearly laughed out loud. There was no predicting how a child's mind worked. "You'll like him. He's a good man." A responsible and usually kind one…but rigid and unjust sometimes, too.

Ever since their earlier conversation, old wounds that Jan believed were healed had begun to throb. This must be the psychological equivalent of the scar tissue her father used to complain about. A firefighter injured on the job, he'd chafed at working a desk position and pushed himself to get back into shape. Under stress, however, his old injuries had flared up. Worse, the damage from smoke inhalation had contributed to the lung disease that killed him.

"What will he do with Smidge?" demanded Kimmie.

Depending on how she described the situation, Jan realized she could easily put Zack in a bad light. But while this might feel to her like a battle for her daughter's affections, she knew if she indulged in a me-against-him mentality, the loser would be Kimmie.

"He promised to take the kitten to a shelter that will find a good home for it," Jan said. "It's a place Mrs. Humphreys recommended."

"He could keep it and let me visit."

"There'll be other kittens." That weak response was the best she could devise at the moment. Time to change the subject. "Where do you want to go for lunch on Sunday?"

"Is what's-her-name coming, too?"

"Berry."

"That's a funny name. Like a fruit."

"It's lucky they didn't name her Banana!" They shared a chuckle. "Don't tell her that, you'll hurt her feelings. And no, she's not coming. She's singing with a church group."

"Oh." Kimmie considered. "How about pancakes? You never let me have pancakes for lunch."

No harm in that, for once. "I'll suggest it to him," Jan said. "Okay?"

"I guess so." More intense concentration was followed by "What do I call him?"

Important question, to which Jan had no easy answer. "What do you want to call him?"

"He said his name is Zack. I can call him that."

Jan nodded and began clearing the dishes. If Zack preferred to be called dad or daddy, he could tell Kimmie himself.

That had gone well, she supposed. There'd be more questions and emotional ups and downs ahead, no doubt. Still, if she and Zack maintained their delicate balance, eventually the idea of having a daddy who lived nearby would begin to seem normal to their daughter.

Jan doubted being around Zack would ever feel normal to her. There was too much hurt and disappointment. The yearning she still felt, against her will, to touch him and see that special smile light his eyes—the loving support she'd needed so badly and the memory of how he'd given it to someone else—only made things worse.

How many hundreds of times had she mentally relived that night at the hospital, the one that had destroyed everything? She'd read the doctor's orders in disbelief. This world-renowned cardiologist had prescribed what she believed to be an overdose of medication.

Certain the nursing supervisor would recognize the mistake as she did, Jan had gone in search of the woman. To her shock, Mrs. Snodgrass had reacted with fury. "You should know better than to question Dr. Ringgel's orders. You're barely out of nursing school!"

Jan had offered to show the order to the cardiology resident, who'd been sleeping in the on-call room after a long shift. The supervisor had refused to wake him.

Confused, Jan had asked another nurse what she thought. Although the woman agreed the dose was too large, she'd explained Mrs. Snodgrass had once countermanded Dr. Ringgel's orders and suffered a reprimand that delayed her promotion to supervisor.

Afraid of causing injury, Jan had dredged up her courage and put in a call to the cardiologist. When he answered, she could hear crowd noises at the background. "You're interrupting my granddaughter's wedding reception to question my orders?" he'd roared. "You're a little nobody. Follow my instructions or I'll have you dismissed!"

Once again she'd gone to Mrs. Snodgrass, who'd become even angrier on learning Jan had disturbed Dr. Ringgel. "Where did you earn your medical degree, Nurse Garcia?" she'd demanded. "Administer the medication *now*."

Later, Jan had wished over and over that she'd stood her ground. Had she been more experienced and confident, she could have insisted she was too uncomfortable to give the dose and that the nursing supervisor administer it herself. But she'd been only twenty-two and accustomed to obeying her superiors, and had begun doubting her own judgment.

So she'd followed orders and nearly killed the patient.

She'd been horrified and guilt-stricken. When Dr. Ringgel denied speaking to her and Mrs. Snodgrass claimed Jan hadn't mentioned the situation, she'd been stunned but certain the hospital records would back her up. Only they didn't.

The other nurse hadn't dared open her mouth. When Zack insisted Jan must be lying, she'd felt utterly betrayed.

For weeks after breaking their engagement she'd been trapped in a haze of disbelief, which gradually yielded to anger. When she discovered she was pregnant, despite the fact they'd used contraception, she'd flung the information at Zack. Although she'd brought papers for him to waive his parental rights, she'd hoped he would beg her to take back the ring and marry him.

Instead, he'd signed the papers. No expression of warmth or concern—merely icy acceptance.

Facing an uncertain personal future and a career in shambles, Jan had hired a lawyer with her parents' help. He'd subpoenaed phone records that showed she'd called the doctor. He'd also persuaded the other nurse, who by then had quit in disgust to work at a different facility, to testify about her conversation with Jan that night and about seeing the doctor's wrong dosage.

By the time Kimmie was born, the hospital had quietly settled, providing enough money for Jan's living expenses and part of her master's degree, as well as clearing her name. The doctor, diagnosed in the early stages of dementia, had been allowed to retire and relinquish his medical license. The nursing supervisor had been demoted. If she'd falsified those records herself, she should have been fired, but Jan never found out the rest of the story.

In any event it had been too late for her and Zack. Although she'd persuaded herself she'd made the right decision in keeping Kimmie without his knowledge, the day of reckoning had come at last.

As she loaded the dishwasher and prepared to read with Kimmie, Jan hoped the change in their lives wasn't going to harm her little girl or Zack's stepdaughter, or disrupt the environment at work. With luck, the two of them could keep this matter private, as they'd agreed. Eventually the girls might become friends. Perhaps even feel like sisters.

But she had a suspicion this process wasn't going to be nearly as easy as that.

## Chapter Five

Zack awoke Tuesday morning with a kitten sitting on his face.

*Sitting* might not be the correct term. Falling, pouncing, or possibly stumbling. All he knew was one minute he was performing mental surgery on an endless row of dream patients lying anesthetized in a long operating room, and the next tiny claws dug into his face while fur tickled his nose.

He sneezed and instinctively batted the thing away. A mew of protest brought his startled attention to a small orange-and-white figure trying to right itself while thrashing amid the sheets. Against the dark blue bedding, the creature stood out like a sunburst.

Reaching for it, Zack halted with his hand in midair. His face stung from the piercings, which he assumed were unintentional. Now the kitten appeared to be in fighting mode. The last thing a surgeon needed was deep scratches on his hands.

Sitting up, he stared at the furry invader, trying to figure out how it got here. Technically, the answer was a jump from the floor onto a footstool Berry used to need, then to a chair, and then to the bed.

But he'd firmly closed the downstairs bathroom door.

And that was a steep flight of stairs for such a small creature.

"Berry?" he called.

His daughter's face poked into view in the open doorway. "Oh, there she is!"

"You brought her upstairs?" The answer was obvious. Even though he'd expressly told her the kitten was to stay in the washroom, Zack decided not to press the issue.

Last night when he'd explained about the baby he'd given up for adoption and who wasn't adopted after all, she'd received the news with her usual somberness. When he'd added that Kimmie attended the same school and had rescued the kitten, Berry had frowned.

"I heard about that!" she'd said. "That's where Smidge came from?"

He'd already regretted revealing the little creature's name. "Yes, but she can't stay. You know our rule about pets."

Receiving no response, he'd added that he had asked Kimmie to lunch on Sunday while Berry was singing. Since parents weren't invited to the convalescent home, his absence hadn't seemed to pose a problem.

He must have missed something. Bringing the kitten upstairs constituted an act of rebellion for Berry.

As she crossed the room, her cranberry-colored pajamas flattering the milk-chocolate creaminess of her skin, he noticed with a start how tall she'd grown. Berry came from a tall family: Rima had been five foot eight, and at six foot two, Berry's uncle Edgar had a good four inches on Zack. Berry wasn't there yet, but she must have grown two inches over the summer.

"Good morning, angel." He reached out to hug his daughter but missed. She'd bent to scoop up the kitten.

Holding the little creature, she sat on the edge of the

bed. "I'm keeping her." Was that a trace of defiance? Totally out of character.

"We already discussed that." This wasn't a negotiation. Parents set the rules.

"My room's plenty big. She can sleep with me, and we'll put the litter box in my bathroom." Apparently she'd given this a lot of thought. "You won't know she's there."

*Don't kid yourself.* Zack glanced at the clock. They'd have to rush to get ready for school and work. He had patients tightly scheduled this morning to make time for this afternoon's staff meeting, and Berry shouldn't be late for school, either.

However, an eight-year-old deserved the truth. "I'm coming home at noon to take her to the animal shelter. Like I said, they'll find her a good home."

Berry clutched the kitten to her shoulder. Her fierce expression reminded him of Kimmie's. "*This* is her home."

"We're gone all day." Zack threw off the covers and slid out the other side of the bed. "It's unfair to her. She'll be lonely."

"Roar will watch over her." That was Berry's stuffed lion. "She likes being a mommy."

"Roar is a she?" That was news to him, Zack reflected as he tugged the covers into place.

Berry nodded. "We both love Smidge." She rubbed her cheek over the kitten, which poked a paw into her curly hair. The claw stuck. The more the kitten tried to pull its paw free, the more entangled it became. "Ow!"

Zack gently freed his daughter's hair. "We should get this cut." She'd worn cute, short curls until last spring, when she insisted on letting her hair grow. It was long enough now to braid for special occasions.

"No!" As soon as she could move freely, she drew away.

"Fine. You can let it grow as long as you like." Even though Zack considered longer hair inconvenient, she had a right to choose her hairstyle. Pets were another matter. "But I don't want you to come home expecting to find the kitten here."

"Then I'm not going to school!" Lips quivering, Berry hurried out of the room cradling the animal. Down the hall he heard her door shut, not quite hard enough to constitute a slam.

*This is what comes of doing Jan a favor.* No, that was unfair. He hadn't brought Smidge home for Jan's sake, but for Kimmie's.

Almost certain that despite her words his daughter had the sense to dress for school, Zack showered and put on slacks, a freshly laundered shirt and a sport jacket. In the mirror he saw that his dark blond hair swept across his forehead in the casual style he preferred. What if someone told him he had to get a buzz cut to be more practical?

*I didn't say that.* Keeping an animal in the house was another matter. In addition to the risk of fleas and infections, there'd be the litter box to change, food to monitor, hair balls and fur everywhere and expensive trips to the veterinarian.

His arguments lined up like soldiers on a parade field, Zack went to knock on his daughter's door. To his relief Berry emerged in jeans and a clean T-shirt, her hair damp and combed. From the way she closed the door behind her, he gathered the kitten was inside.

Zack fixed a breakfast of cereal, milk and sliced fruit. Because Berry came from a family with a deadly history of heart disease, he emphasized a healthy diet and exercise even more than he might have otherwise.

After washing her hands at Zack's insistence—he

wasn't taking any chances with that kitten—Berry ate hungrily. Zack wasn't sure whether to mention the cat again or leave the matter alone. He'd already informed her he planned to drive Smidge to the shelter at noon. While she might fuss when she got home and found the kitten gone, Berry would get over it quickly.

He'd buy her a new stuffed animal. Better yet, he'd take her shopping this evening.

Berry set down her spoon. "On Sunday," she announced, "I want to go to Brady's house after we sing."

"Brady's house?" Although Berry sometimes kidded around with the younger boy at church, they weren't close friends. However, he did sing in the choir and his mother, Kate, served as assistant choir director, so they'd both be participating in the special event. "I can try to arrange it, but why?" Zack asked.

"I don't want to meet that other little girl." Worry lines puckered Berry's forehead.

"I wasn't planning to introduce you yet." Zack hadn't thought that far ahead. "But you always said you wanted a brother or sister."

Berry stared at him in horror. "She's not my sister!"

"Not exactly," he agreed, "but…"

"How come she gets a new daddy and I can't even have a kitten?" To his dismay, tears darkened Berry's eyes. His daughter hadn't cried in…well, months, at least.

Zack reached across the table to touch her. She shrugged him off and ducked her head.

His usually easygoing little girl appeared desperately upset. How had this happened? "Berry, I love you more than anything in the world. That doesn't mean I can't…" Zack halted. He'd been about to say there was room in his heart to love them both equally. His better judgment warned the idea wasn't likely to play well.

When patients asked why their older child became distressed at the prospect of a new baby, he often shared an analogy he'd read—imagine how you'd feel if your husband came home and announced he loved you so much he was taking a second wife, but that he had plenty of love for both of you?

"I don't even know this new little girl," Zack amended. "Kimmie isn't the same as you."

Folding her arms, Berry refused to meet his gaze.

Zack had always resolved not to be a parent who yielded to blackmail and Rima had stood firmly beside him on that issue. The few times that Berry, as a toddler, had thrown a tantrum she'd learned in no uncertain terms there'd be a punishment, such as missing her favorite cartoons that evening. She'd quickly backed down.

But this wasn't exactly defiance. The kitten appeared to mean something important to her. Something symbolic.

Struggling to find the key, Zack reflected on what she'd said. *How come she gets a new daddy and I can't even have a kitten?* He was willing to make major changes in his life to get close to Kimmie. Maybe Berry was seeking reassurance he'd willingly sacrifice for her sake, too.

To an adult it wasn't the same thing at all—to a child it might be.

Zack supposed he could give the kitten a twenty-four hour reprieve to allow him time to consider all the angles. *The longer you delay, the more attached Berry will become.* He had to decide now.

"Would you feel better about Kimmie if I let you keep the kitten?" Ignoring the wall clock's reminder to hurry, Zack focused on his daughter.

Biting her lower lip, she nodded.

"Your happiness matters to me," Zack told her. "More than my inconvenience or my concerns about keeping a pet. You'll have to help feed it and clean up. And keep her in the bathroom until she's housebroken."

"The upstairs bathroom is bigger."

"Okay," he said.

"When she grows up we'll close off the living room," Berry said. "So she won't scratch Mommy's furniture."

*She's way ahead of me.* "What made you think of that?"

"Cindy has a kitty."

"Did she mention how often she feeds it and brushes it and…" He broke off. "We can find that stuff on the internet."

"Tonight!"

"It's a plan." Doing research might even prove educational. "Now we'd better hurry."

Berry hopped to her feet. "I love you, Daddy!" She flung her arms around him, then bounced away. "I'll get my backpack."

As he cleared the dishes, Zack wondered if someday, when he had an adolescent daughter wearing outrageous clothes and ditching school, he might not look back on this moment with nostalgia.

In any event he'd learned a lesson: tread carefully with Berry where Kimmie was concerned.


By one-fifteen, when he finished his last appointment for the morning, Zack was grateful he didn't have to run out and take the kitten to the shelter. Before leaving the house, he'd put it in the upstairs bathroom with plenty of food and water.

If anyone had asked him a few days ago whether he'd be adopting a cat, he'd have laughed at the idea. But fatherhood required a degree of flexibility, just so long as one didn't bend on matters of principle.

He ate a sandwich in the cafeteria. Then he swung by

Jan's office, hoping to talk before the two-o'clock staff meeting.

He found her organizing her notes on the computer. "Hi," she said distractedly. "Zack. Good. Close the door."

She had something on her mind. Was it about Kimmie's reaction? Zack swung into a chair, and waited while Jan closed and printed her file.

Dark hair fell smoothly over the collar of her lavender suit jacket, and a delicate gold bracelet emphasized the slimness of her wrist. Despite her collected appearance, she had a worried air as she faced him. "Dr. T just emailed that Samantha Forrest plans to join us. Why would a pediatrician care about the egg-donor program?"

Good question. "She counsels a group of teen mothers," Zack said.

"I don't see how that's relevant."

"Neither do I," he admitted. "Just thinking out loud."

"She's the wife of the administrator, and I understand her nickname is Fightin' Sam." Jan had clearly done her research. "Is she a pain in the neck?"

"Can be," Zack had to admit. "If she gets her nose in a twist over something, she's like a bulldog."

"A bulldog with a twisted nose? Sounds painful." Jan wrinkled her own nose, which was cute and decidedly un-bulldog-like. "I hate office politics."

"I don't know if I hate them. I'm just lousy at them." Since Zack had nothing further to say on the subject, he posed the question uppermost in his mind. "How did Kimmie take the news?"

Jan's expression softened. "She's okay with it. Do you object to her eating pancakes for lunch?"

Normally, he would. But Kimmie wasn't Berry, whose mother and grandparents had died young of heart disease.

"I've heard rave reviews of a restaurant called Waffle Heaven. Guess this is my chance to try it."

Jan looked relieved. "That'll help break the ice. How did Berry react?"

Complicated question. "At first, she didn't say much. She holds things inside." Zack pictured his daughter's face, barely a muscle moving as she'd listened to him.

"She's been through a lot." Jan studied him sympathetically. "It's wonderful that she has you."

"I'm lucky to have *her*." Zack had bonded with the little girl from the moment they met. Literally.

"Does she have other relatives? Grandparents?"

"Deceased." He chose not to be specific. Rima and her family were private territory. "Just an uncle who's young and unmarried. We get together on holidays."

"What about your parents?" Jan sounded hesitant, and no wonder. The elder Sargents hadn't exactly welcomed her as his fiancée. Not that they'd acted crazy about Rima, either, but they'd accepted her once she became his wife. As their only grandchild, Berry received hugs and gifts on appropriate occasions, but hardly the outpouring of devotion he'd seen in other grandparents.

"They've never been the warm, fuzzy type," Zack said. He suddenly realized he'd never told them about the baby he'd relinquished. There was another touchy issue to be handled.

"So initially she didn't show much reaction. What about later?" Impressive, how Jan zeroed in on the key issue.

Zack wasn't sure how to describe what had happened. "She latched on to the kitten. She asked how come Kimmie got a new daddy and she couldn't even have a pet."

Jan smiled.

"What?" Zack said.

"You folded."

"We compromised." That sounded more dignified.

"On what?"

"On me folding."

She chuckled. "Good for you. I'm relieved Smidge has a home."

"Glad you approve." The issues weren't settled, however. "Berry calls Kimmie 'the other little girl' and refused to meet her."

"You're all she's got, and now she has to share you," Jan said. "It's natural for her to feel threatened."

He acknowledged the truth of that observation. "Kimmie wasn't angry about my being gone all her life?"

"More confused than angry." Jan gave a start as her cell phone beeped. "That's my alarm. It's time to leave for the staff meeting. Think there's any harm in our riding up the elevator together?" They were gathering in a small fourth-floor auditorium used for lectures and continuing education.

"Your receptionist already saw me come in, so the gossip's in the wind." Caroline Carter was a chatty twentysomething who had previously been assigned to a private—and isolated—medical office. Now, as a receptionist and secretary to Jan and several other staff members in a ground-floor location, she was perfectly positioned to follow all the hospital news.

"I suspected as much. When I mentioned Dr. Forrest, Caroline was more than happy to fill me in." Jan collected a clipboard with her notes. "While I dislike gossip, I don't want to walk blindly into a lion's den."

"I'm on your side." Not that Zack wielded much power around here. "So is Dr. Tartikoff. He was eager to have you on board."

"Nevertheless, he enjoys stirring things up." Jan took a deep breath. "Well, nobody promised this job would be easy. Ready?"

"You bet."

# Chapter Six

*Stay calm. Be friendly. Listen actively.* Jan ran over that
mantra as she greeted the staff members—eight, plus
her—in the classroom-size auditorium, which had about
thirty steeply ascending seats. Given how few people were
present at this initial meeting, she'd have preferred to sit
around a conference table, but Dr. T had arranged for
them to meet here.

Perhaps, by placing her at a podium, he meant to demonstrate she was the person in charge. To her way of thinking this ought to be a cooperative venture. But perhaps
there wasn't a suitable boardroom.

As the attendees exchanged greetings and took their
seats, Jan assessed the participants. Embryologist Alec
Denny was his usual easygoing self, while the hospital
attorney, Tony Franco, mentioned how much his wife,
Kate, had enjoyed meeting Jan at the school yesterday.

Financial counselor Melissa Everhart and IVF coordinator Karen Wiggins were both eager to get the donor
program underway. The administrator, obstetrician Mark
Rayburn, greeted her with low-key warmth and sat next
to Tony rather than with his wife, who'd chosen a higher
tier. Although Jan considered her a wild card, Samantha
Forrest had shaken hands and greeted her politely. Still,
the sharp-featured blonde pediatrician hadn't explained

why she was here, and several of the others cast puzzled glances in her direction.

As expected, Owen Tartikoff took the podium for an introduction, his russet hair and cinnamon eyes giving him a deceptively mild appearance. "You've all met Jan Garcia. As you may know, she and I worked together in Boston. Since then she's been assistant director of an egg-donor program in Houston. She was my top choice to fill this post."

Standing at the side, Jan felt a nervous tingling in her hands. *Please don't let me drop these papers.*

"I'd like to provide a little background, so we don't lose sight of the bigger picture." Owen spoke easily, without notes. "The first fertilized egg was successfully transferred from one woman to another in July 1983 about an hour's drive from here, at Harbor, UCLA Medical Center. Today, the process is performed all over the world but many countries impose restrictions. Most commonly, they limit or ban paying the donors."

On an upper tier, Samantha leaned forward. Since she didn't work in the fertility field, perhaps this was new to her, Jan mused.

"That creates a shortage," Dr. T said. "Donating eggs is a complex, invasive procedure, and except for close relatives, few women will undergo it purely from altruism. The U.S. has no such restrictions on egg donation and therefore no such shortage. As a result, women from all over the world come here to undergo fertility treatments. And while there are many egg-donor programs in Southern California, we believe there's an unmet demand. We've already had inquiries both from within our program and from outside patients, because of our excellent reputation."

*Stop now,* Jan commanded mentally, but he went right

on talking. She'd forgotten how much Dr. T loved an audience.

"We must never forget we're dealing with people's children, not merely bits of tissue," Owen continued. "Some of you remember the scandal just down the road from here, at UC Irvine, in the mid-nineties, when doctors were accused of stealing eggs from fertility patients and implanting them in other women, who believed the eggs had been donated. You can imagine the heartbreak and the lawsuits that resulted, and two doctors fled the country. While I'm sure no one here would deliberately commit such a reprehensible act, we must have safeguards to ensure nothing like that happens by accident."

Tony nodded. Samantha showed no reaction. What *was* her issue?

"On that note, I implant you in the capable hands of Jan Garcia." With a flash of his deep-etched dimple, Dr. T stepped down.

Great. He'd just filled everyone's ears with horror stories and now Jan had to follow that.

Taking a deep breath, she walked to the podium.

BECAUSE HE KNEW JAN so well, Zack registered the tension in her stride and the taut edge to her voice. Beyond that, however, she came across as coolly professional.

Quite a challenge, given the way Dr. T had brought in controversy right from the start. As if anyone in this room needed reminding about the UCI scandal, which had received worldwide publicity.

Jan calmly provided an overview of what lay ahead. Like every other clinic, this one needed to decide on its rules and establish its procedures. Also, by law, clinics were required to send statistical information each year to the Society for Assisted Reproductive Technology and the federal Centers for Disease Control. This information would be released to the public in reports showing pregnancy rates.

"Our first task is to decide on some key protocols. For example, what standards will we use to screen egg donors? Also, will we set up a shared-cycle IVF program? That's something I encourage, by the way," Jan added.

"Excuse me." Samantha Forrest stood without waiting to be recognized. From her hunched shoulders to her fisted hands, she appeared braced for a fight. "What about protecting the egg donors from exploitation?"

So *that* was her issue. Understandable, Zack supposed, in light of her work with troubled young women who might see egg donation as an easy way to make money.

"I'm glad you raised that point, Dr. Forrest." Jan showed no trace of alarm. "Please elaborate. I want to be sure we take your concerns into account."

"Well…" The pediatrician blinked, as if caught off guard by the pleasant reception. *Good for you, Jan.* "We have to be sure they're fully informed about the tests and examinations they'll undergo, the hormones they'll receive, the possibility of long-term physical effects, not to mention the emotional impact. How will they feel years later when they realize other women are raising their babies?"

Jan jotted notes on a pad. "Excellent. That's the kind of input I'm looking for. Would you be willing to serve on a team to prepare an information sheet we'll give to prospective donors?"

Dr. Forrest glanced toward her husband, who kept his gaze fixed on Jan. They were raising adopted triplets, which Zack doubted left much spare time. Still, if she truly cared about this matter… "Sure."

"Thank you. And naturally, we'll do a full psychological workup on all donors," Jan continued.

Samantha hadn't finished. "Also, I understand they don't get paid until the eggs are harvested. That's a lot of time for them to invest on speculation, so to speak."

"No more than many job candidates invest in seeking employment," Jan countered in a level tone. "Also, the payment is substantial—usually about five thousand dollars per cycle."

"That's enough to entice a young girl, but it may not feel so great when she's older and looks back on her decision," the pediatrician persisted.

Realizing this topic could sidetrack the whole session, Zack decided to speak up. "If we paid young women before they underwent the egg harvesting, we'd be facing a host of problems." His voice echoed slightly in the conference room.

As everyone turned toward him, he caught a trace of surprise on several faces. Except for his grant-program proposal, Zack usually stayed in the background. But he wasn't about to let Dr. Forrest or anyone else throw the plans for an egg-donor program off course.

"Please go on," Jan said.

"First, some individuals could take advantage of the program by getting paid for their time when they don't seriously intend to donate," Zack said. "Second, we can't charge fertility patients for eggs they don't receive, so where would the payments come from?"

Sam folded her arms. Not persuaded.

"The third danger is that fertile women who fantasize about having multiple babies—and I'm sure many of us have encountered those—will sign up, make it through to the hormonal stage, and then intentionally get pregnant with all those eggs inside."

"What would stop them from doing that anyway?" Sam shot back.

"Psychological screening," Jan reminded her.

"They can manipulate that," the pediatrician insisted.

"There's also the high cost of medical care for multiple babies," Zack said. "If we pay them without requiring that we harvest the eggs, that's a major added incentive. True, it might not be a lot of money in the long-term, but some women could see it as getting their wish and having us help fund it."

Jan smoothly picked up the ball. "You've raised an important concern we have with egg donors. There can be as many as fifteen eggs per cycle, or more. They must agree to abstain from sex two weeks before and after ovulating, because we can't be certain we've harvested all the eggs. One woman in Houston ignored that restriction and even after being harvested got pregnant with quads. Just imagine if a woman deliberately became pregnant with a dozen babies. It would be a medical and moral disaster."

Dr. Sam considered this aspect. "That's a good point."

"We're only at the start of our discussions," Jan said, "and I appreciate all the input. Now, let's touch on some other matters because I know you all have obligations elsewhere today."

In the front row, Zack saw Dr. T's head bob with approval. Jan had taken Samantha's concerns into account, finessed the challenge to her leadership and kept the meeting on track.

Zack was proud of her.

DESPITE HER CONCERN that Samantha might drop another bomb during the session, Jan managed to run through her list of topics, field questions and wrap things up by three-thirty, as planned. There'd be many more sessions ahead, but most would involve only a few participants with specific areas of expertise.

After she thanked everyone and stepped down, Dr. T reached her in a flash. "Good job. When do you anticipate we can begin recruitment?"

"Next spring. Possibly earlier," Jan said.

"Excellent." And he was off, striding out as if he had an office full of women waiting for him, which might be true.

Others congratulated her on a job well done. Jan promised to contact each of them to schedule further talks.

Dr. Forrest hung back. Waiting her chance for a more lengthy discussion, or would it be an argument?

Zack's presence bolstered Jan's sense of security. She wanted to thank him for taking some of the heat, but she couldn't do that in front of Samantha. And, unable to outwait the pediatrician, he bowed out politely. "I've got patients at four. Great job, Jan."

"Thank you." She kept her tone crisp and courteous. And tried not to show how her stomach tensed as his strong figure disappeared through the doorway.

Feeling as if she faced a firing squad, Jan shifted her attention to Samantha. "I appreciate your volunteering to help with the information sheet. Being supportive to our donors is vital."

The pediatrician shook back her wavy blond hair. Tall and forceful, she had a larger-than-life presence. "I'm not opposed to the program, in case you got that impression."

"Not at all. I've heard good things about your counseling program. It's wonderful you're willing to advocate for others." Jan considered suggesting they sit down, but decided to stay mobile in case the discussion took a heated turn.

"I sympathize with the recipients as well as the donors," the pediatrician noted. "It came as a shock when I learned I was undergoing premature ovarian failure and couldn't have a baby of my own. Because of my medical history, I was advised against taking hormones, so I couldn't use donor eggs."

"I understand you adopted triplets."

Sam's expression mellowed. "Sometimes life gives us what we need, whether we deserve it or not. I just wanted to let you know that, while I sympathize with egg recipients, someone has to speak for the donors."

"It's good to have those checks and balances." Jan meant that sincerely. "A good critic is precious."

"I can see why Owen wanted you on board." Sam reached out to shake hands. "You're an asset to the hospital."

"Thanks." Jan watched her go with a profound sense of relief.

She'd weathered a challenge. Undoubtedly, there'd be others, but she could deal with them. And she was genuinely grateful for input like Samantha's.

Still, it felt good that Zack was willing to speak up for her. Jan only hoped they could work together as smoothly with the girls.

ON SUNDAY MORNING, she awoke feeling anxious. *Today's the day Kimmie has lunch with her father. What if something goes wrong?* Maybe she should call Zack and tell him she was coming along, or at least sitting in another part of the restaurant.

He'd insist that she trust him. And he'd be right.

She glanced at the clock. Nine-thirty! She hadn't expected to doze this late.

Rising, she went to check on Kimmie. Her daughter usually fixed her own cereal, and Jan assumed she'd find

Kimmie playing in her bedroom or watching cartoons. No sign of her in either place.

Heart thudding, she hurried to check the door. Unlocked.

Where would Kimmie go? She wasn't allowed out of the apartment without permission, and then only to play in the tot lot visible from the front window.

Jan peered out. In the morning mist, no little shapes moved on the playground.

*She must have gone to get the paper.* The newspaper was delivered to a box near the steps leading to the second floor. Kimmie might have been eager to read the comics.

Jan retrieved her robe, grabbed her keys and cell phone, and went out into the foggy morning. At the foot of the stairs she found the newspaper still in its box. No little girl around.

Should she call the landlord? She doubted he'd do anything except get angry at being disturbed on a Sunday morning. And she hadn't met her neighbors beyond a passing hello. Was it too soon to call the police?

As she stood there debating, a small figure came around the corner of the building. With a burst of relief, Jan recognized her nightgown-clad daughter, arms overflowing with a large gray-and-white cat.

"Kimmie!" Jan kept her voice low to avoid disturbing the neighbors. "You scared me half to death."

The little girl regarded her apologetically. "I'm sorry, Mommy. I came out to get the paper. I heard her meowing."

Jan took a closer look. "That's a him. He's a tomcat and that's what they do. They yowl." Some irresponsible owner had neglected to get the cat neutered, which meant he was on the prowl, prone to fighting with other toms and almost impossible to keep indoors.

"He's hungry," her daughter protested. "We have to feed him."

"If we do that, he'll come around all the time." Much as Jan wished she could help the animal, getting involved could only cause trouble. "He looks well fed to me. Kimmie, please put him down."

Her daughter might have argued further had the cat not begun squirming. Reluctantly she squatted and set him on the ground. He rubbed against her and gazed upward. "See? He loves me."

"I'll bet he has an owner. That's why he's so comfortable around people." While Jan didn't see a collar, it might have fallen off. Besides, in a complex like this, she had no doubt plenty of people would feed a stray. "Have you had breakfast?"

"No."

"Bet you're hungry."

"Yeah." Giving the cat one last pat, Kimmie rose with a sigh.

Jan said a silent prayer of thanks while collecting the newspaper. "Don't ever come out here by yourself again," she added. "There's a reason we have rules."

"I didn't see any strangers," the little girl protested as they went inside the apartment.

"Thank goodness for that."

"Are you going to tell my daddy?" Kimmie's voice trembled.

Halfway to the kitchen, Jan halted. "I don't see any reason to. Why do you ask?"

"Allie's daddy spanks her when she's bad." Standing in the middle of the living room, she hugged herself protectively.

"Zack isn't going to spank you." Although they hadn't discussed discipline, Jan couldn't imagine him doing such a thing. When Kimmie was too small to reason with, Jan had occasionally used a well-placed swat on the rear end to short-circuit a tantrum, but never hard enough to do more than startle the girl. Now she used explanations combined with loss of privileges.

"Are you mad at me?"

"No. I'm glad you care about animals. But we can't save the whole world." Jan washed her hands and made sure her daughter did the same. "Now, let's have our cereal and see what's in the comics."

A few hours later, after a leisurely session reading the comics and a beautifying bout in the bathroom, the little cat-rescuer was transformed into a pretty girl clad in a sunny-yellow dress with puffed sleeves, patent-leather shoes and white socks with yellow ruffles. Kimmie didn't even protest when Jan curled her dark hair at the ends so it formed a sleek curtain around her shoulders, with yellow bows securing it at the temples.

"You look beautiful," Jan told her daughter.

"You, too, Mommy."

"Thanks." She'd put on a pink wrap skirt with a rose knit top and a rosette clip in her hair. Jan planned on shopping while her daughter was gone, and she liked to look her best. You never knew who you might run into while out in public.

The doorbell made her jump. Zack must wear rubber-soled shoes, she reflected with a flash of annoyance, as if he'd violated some unspoken agreement by not giving her more warning.

She and Kimmie exchanged here-we-go glances, and Jan went to open the door.

# Chapter Seven

The uncertainty in Zack's eyes as he stood in the doorway reminded Jan of their first date. After months of kidding around and sharing coffee breaks at the hospital where they both worked, she hadn't expected him to act so nervous when he picked her up to attend a street festival. But then, her skin had prickled and her breath caught, too.

The same way she felt now.

He hadn't come to see her, of course. And her nerves were for her daughter's sake, not her own. *Or they ought to be.*

"Come in. Kimmie's ready," she said unnecessarily, since he could see the little girl standing with hands clasped in front of her yellow dress.

"Kimmie. Hi." With a nod to Jan, Zack stepped into the room. Jan could see him registering the small space and shabby furnishings, or was she picking up on her own insecurities? Almost at once, his attention was riveted on her daughter. On *their* daughter. "I'm sorry I didn't introduce myself properly when we first met. I'm…"

Guessing he was uncertain what name to use, Jan said, "Kimmie suggested calling you Zack. Is that all right?"

Disappointment flickered across his face, vanishing quickly. "Sure. Maybe when we're better acquainted… Well, she looks adorable in that outfit, Jan."

"She was very cooperative."

Kimmie stared down at her shoes.

Zack spoke gently. "I guess this is scary, going to lunch with a man you've barely met."

She still avoided his gaze.

Jan took pity on them both. "How's Smidge?" That was sure to be a conversation starter.

Zack seized on the topic. "We bought her a toy mouse. You should see her jump around playing with it."

"I bet she's cute." Kimmie raised her eyes at last. "I know a tomcat. He's big and gray and I named him Gorilla."

"Kimmie!" Jan reproved. "He probably already has a name and an owner."

"He's lonely. He likes me."

"I'm sure he does." Zack moved ahead smoothly. "We're going to a restaurant called Waffle Heaven. I hear they have great pancakes."

"Did you make a reservation?" Jan asked. "Sunday brunches tend to get crowded."

"Forgot." He took out his phone. "I'll see how long the wait is." He found the number and placed the call. "Half hour. Not too bad."

"Is your phone new?" Kimmie was fascinated with electronic devices, especially since Jan limited her access.

"Yes. Hey, look at this cool app for kids." He tapped the screen a few times and then handed it to her.

"Wow!" She was instantly absorbed.

Jan fetched a couple of children's magazines. "You might want to take these along also. It's hard for two people to read a story on a cell phone."

"Thanks." He reached out, his hand brushing hers, and warmth flooded Jan as their eyes met in shared understanding.

Breaking the contact, Zack flipped through the pages. "Animal stories. I should subscribe to this. Berry would love it."

"It's an excellent magazine," Kimmie said in her most grown-up fashion. "I'll get my purse."

"Sure." As she darted from the room, Zack said, "She sounds almost like an adult."

"Sometimes," Jan admitted. "Her moods can change in a snap. Good thing you have experience with girls. Speaking of which, how does Berry feel about you taking Kimmie to lunch?"

"Hard to tell." He rolled up the magazines. "After the choir performance, she's riding home with Kate and Brady Franco. Hopefully she'll be too busy to think about what's going on with me."

"I hope so, too." Jan broke off as her daughter returned. "Have a great time, you guys." She hugged the little girl.

Kimmie wiggled away. "You'll mess up my hair, Mommy."

"We can't have that." Jan smiled. Usually her daughter didn't care about such things. But now she had a man in her life.

*A father.* Jan felt a wave of regret. *I wish I hadn't had to keep them apart.*

"I expect to have her home by three," Zack said.

"Can I see Smidge?" When he hesitated, Kimmie added, "Please?"

"We can stop by my house after lunch," Zack conceded. "If that's all right with your mother."

"Okay." Jan tried not to think about how Kimmie might react to seeing that big, beautiful house.

Zack escorted their daughter out the door. They'd have a great time, Jan told herself. And, she recalled, she had only a few hours to shop for something to spruce up her decor and then buy groceries.

A few minutes later, emerging from the bedroom with her purse, she saw her cell phone sitting on the coffee table. Puzzled, she went to pick it up, and realized it wasn't hers.

It was Zack's. Kimmie must have set it there and he hadn't noticed.

Now what? If she took it to the restaurant, that meant crashing his date with their daughter. Being alone together was important for them. On the other hand, suppose the hospital or Berry needed to reach him?

After a moment's reflection, Jan decided to take the phone with her. If it rang, she could suggest the caller contact him at the restaurant, or she would run over there herself.

It was only a few hours. People used to get along just fine without being constantly available.

After leaving a note on the door about the phone in case Zack stopped back, Jan hurried out on her errands.

So MUCH FOR BEING alone with Kimmie, Zack thought with amused frustration as they sat in the restaurant's crowded waiting area. Reading aloud and making funny voices had been a great idea to pass the time. A little too great. Before long, a restless toddler had wandered over from a family group, soon to be joined by his older sister. Shortly afterward, a boy who'd been racing around driving everyone crazy joined them.

When the hostess finally called out, "Dr. Sargent, party of two," he closed the magazine with a trace of guilt. "Sorry, kids. I'm sure it has a happy ending."

"The kittens find their way home," Kimmie reassured them.

"She called you doctor. Are you a pediatrician?" one of the mothers asked. "You have a way with kids."

"Thanks. I'm an obstetrician. I do have a way with babies." Pleased by the woman's comment, Zack guided Kimmie through the restaurant. The smells of pancakes, waffles, syrup and chocolate were rapidly canceling his intention of sticking to healthier fare.

Because of the importance of a proper diet for Berry, he kept himself on the same restrictions. Good for his waistline, but he missed indulging once in a while.

After a waitress handed them menus and departed, Kimmie asked, "What's a waffle?"

It hadn't occurred to him that she didn't know. "They're like pancakes only they're thicker and have little dents in them to hold the syrup."

On the menu, Kimmie pointed to a picture of a waffle topped with nuts, syrup and whipped cream. "What's that?"

Zack read the caption. "Walnut Maple Surprise." He indicated another. "That's the Pineapple Express."

"I love pineapple!" Her voice rang with excitement.

"Then pineapple it is. Unless you'd prefer the Banana Pecan Special?"

"I like bananas, too." She sounded worried, as if making the wrong choice might have dire consequences.

"We could get both and split them." While he'd prefer the walnut maple, that wasn't the point.

"Yay!" Kimmie said. "I mean, thank you."

What a polite little girl. Even though she had his eyes and Jan's dark hair, Zack felt as if he were taking someone else's daughter to lunch. With Berry, the connection had been instantaneous.

Late one afternoon, striding toward his car in the Los Angeles hospital parking lot, he'd heard a woman calling frantically and seen a toddler galloping toward him, her tiny black pigtails bouncing. "Whoa!" Zack had caught her in a gentle grip. "Okay if I pick you up?"

"Yes! Yes!" The exuberant child had practically flung herself into his arms.

"Ups-a-daisy." As he'd lifted the toddler to carry her to her mother, he'd felt a jolt of tenderness. As if he'd met her before, or as if they'd been destined to meet.

When he restored the tot to her mother, Zack had recognized Rima as a woman he'd seen in the hospital waiting room a few times—probably a patient. He must have seen Berry there as well, but that didn't fully explain the sense of connection.

Rima had been grateful and apologetic, explaining her heart condition prevented her from running after her daughter. As Zack watched them drive off, a sense of loss had washed over him.

A few days previously another nurse had told him that Jan, who was about five months pregnant, was expecting a girl. Zack realized he'd been dreaming about that child, and somehow an image of Berry had sneaked into his subconscious, standing in for the unborn daughter. Just a quirk of his psyche, perhaps, but he'd felt as if she and he were already a family.

A few days later, spotting Berry and Rima in the waiting room, Zack had stopped to chat. Impulsively he'd invited them to a children's art fair he'd seen advertised.

Lonely and hurt by what felt like Jan's betrayal, Zack had quickly grown attached to Rima and Berry. Had he not met them, maybe he'd have tried harder to win Jan's forgiveness three months later when he learned of her innocence in the medication error. Their lives might have taken an entirely different course. But what would have happened to Berry?

"I changed my mind. That's what I want." Kimmie pointed to a picture of a waffle with chocolate and whipped cream. "Okay, Zack?"

He was here to make friends, not enforce a health code. "Sure." *If I were your real father, I'd tell you to eat something that at least pretends to be good for you.*

Only he wasn't yet her real father. And, as Kimmie plopped down the menu and stared past him, he could tell she knew it, too.

VIEWING THE DEPARTMENT store's home-decor section filled Jan with longing. Graceful couches in bright colors, gleaming parquet tables and cabinets, a charming dresser with fairy-tale stencils... She couldn't afford this stuff. Instead, she bought some cheerful throw pillows that were on sale.

Later, at the Suncrest Market, she followed her list around aisles that were just starting to become familiar. She was loading her purchases into the cooler in her trunk when an unfamiliar ring sounded in her purse. Zack's phone!

As she took it out, she checked the time. A little past one-thirty. Were he and Kimmie still at the restaurant?

She pressed the button. "Dr. Sargent's phone."

"Oh." The woman on the other end sounded surprised. "Who is this, please?"

How awkward. And disappointing. *You idiot. You should have considered he might have a girlfriend.* "This is Jan Garcia from the hospital. We had a little mix-up with our phones."

"Oh, Jan!" Someone she knew? "It's Kate Franco."

Relief yielded to concern. "Is Berry all right?"

"She's fine. Well, except for being unusually cranky. I've never seen her this way." Kate's voice had a frazzled edge. "We finished the performance early, and she and Brady have been squabbling ever since. She's demanding to go home this instant."

Now what? Jan and Zack had agreed not to say any more than necessary about the situation, so she couldn't go into detail as to his whereabouts. "He had some errands to run, so he may not be reachable yet. Why don't I pick up Berry? I'll make sure she gets home safely. I have to drop off his phone anyway."

Then it occurred to her she and Berry hadn't met. The little girl might be understandably reluctant to leave with a stranger. *And Kate's going to think Zack and I are involved.*

Nothing to be done about that.

"Wonderful!" Kate's effusive response didn't leave room for backpedaling. "My baby's fussing and Tony's out playing golf, so he can't drive her. I'd appreciate it so much."

"I'll be right over, if you'll give me directions."

A few minutes later, Jan was on her way.

MAKING POLITE CONVERSATION with a seven-year-old strained Zack's mental agility more than he'd expected. After they ordered, he asked a series of questions to which she gave shorter and shorter replies. Yes, she missed her friends in Texas. No, she didn't eat out often. Yes, she liked her teacher.

Then they sat listening to the surrounding clink of china and chatter of voices. Happy families, close couples, people who conversed without hesitation.

"Is there anything you'd like to ask me?" Zack waited for Kimmie to pose the painful questions. Why didn't you marry my mommy? Why did you raise another little girl instead of me? Why are you here now? Instead, she played with her cutlery and opened packets of sugar, which she dumped into her milk.

"Do you do that at home?" he asked.

"We don't have these paper things." She tore another one, spilling sugar on the table. A sideways glance told him she was monitoring his reaction—testing him.

"If you don't do it at home, please don't do it here," he said.

She made a face but stopped opening packages. Mercifully, the waitress chose that moment to appear with their orders.

The platters looked enormous. "Do you want me to cut up your waffle for you?" Zack asked.

Kimmie regarded the piled-high confection in front of her. "I can do it."

"Tuck your napkin into your collar," Zack warned. "You don't want to splatter chocolate on your dress."

"I'm not a baby!" Her lower lip protruded.

Picking up his own napkin, he stuck it into his shirt collar. "Does that make me a baby?"

She cracked a smile. "It looks silly."

He waited.

"Okay." She did the same.

As Kimmie sawed earnestly at her waffle, Zack instinctively reached over but then dropped his hand. Berry always let him help if she needed it, but this was a different little girl. Very different. Berry would never stuff large chunks of food in her mouth and smear chocolate across her face without wiping it off. He tried his best to ignore the mess.

Kimmie did look cute with those smudges. And she radiated pleasure as she dug into her food. "Mmm, good!"

"It is," Zack agreed. He was enjoying his maple waffle.

"Makes me thirsty!" Grabbing for her glass, Kimmie didn't take into account the slippery chocolate on her hand. As if in slow motion the glass tipped, seemed to hang in midair for a second and then dumped milk all over the table. It soaked the container of sugar packets, flowed around the little pitchers of extra syrup and surged across the tablecloth.

Anger flashed through Zack. How embarrassing! Kimmie should have been more careful.

Large green eyes stared at him in fright. Although he hadn't spoken, she'd registered his fury. "I'm sorry, Zack."

As quickly as it had flared, his rage faded. She was only seven. And he didn't want to be like his father, quick to lash out with harsh words that left scars. "It was an accident."

"You're mad at me." Her chin quivered.

Zack began sopping up milk with his napkin. "You know what?"

Kimmie shook her head.

"My dad used to blow his temper whenever I did anything wrong. It made me scared of him. I don't want you to be scared of me."

Her lips firmed. No telling what she was thinking.

A waitress hurried over. "I'll clean that up for you. We'll get a fresh tablecloth."

"If you could lay down a towel and bring more napkins, we'll make do," Zack told her. "And another glass of milk, please."

"Of course." As she left, Zack made a mental note to leave an extra-large tip.

"You couldn't drink that milk anyway. It was loaded with sugar," he told Kimmie. "Now you get a fresh glass."

"Really?" She blinked at him. "For free?"

"I'll pay for it. This isn't the restaurant's fault." Zack

glanced at her plate. "You got some in your waffle. How does it taste?"

Kimmie took a bite. "Milky. But yum!"

By the time the waitress restored order to their table, Kimmie had relaxed. With a new glass of milk and a clean napkin in place, she ate happily.

"So, are there any questions you want to ask me?" Zack hadn't forgotten his query earlier. Maybe now she'd be more comfortable with him.

Kimmie put down her fork. "You're a doctor, right?"

"That I am," he confirmed.

"Do you fix animals or just people?"

"Just people." Not as naive a question as it might appear. Rural doctors had once treated valuable farm animals as well as humans, and until recently, medical students had practiced surgical techniques on dogs and other living creatures. "Doctors specialize in one or the other. Animal doctors are called veterinarians."

"Why did you pick people?" Kimmie asked.

"I guess that's the way I was brought up," Zack conceded. "My grandfather was a preacher and my father was principal of a private high school. They emphasized service to others. To other people, I mean."

"I like serving to animals," Kimmie replied earnestly.

On the verge of responding it wasn't the same thing, Zack realized Kimmie had every right to her opinion. And that many people would agree with her. "So I've seen."

They moved on to discussing Smidge and her adjustment to her new household. Somewhere along the line, it occurred to Zack they weren't struggling to find topics of conversation anymore.

They'd turned a corner. It might be only one in a series of corners, but he was grateful they'd made it past the first bend in the road.

## Chapter Eight

Tony and Kate Franco's home sat atop a bluff. From the driveway Jan caught a glimpse of the harbor—not directly below, but close enough for her to make out the white triangles of sailboats and the colorful splash of catamarans gliding through the sunlight.

She rang the bell. After a moment Kate answered, her brown hair askew and two-year-old Tara on her shoulder. "Oh, good! You got here fast."

"I came right from the supermarket." Jan followed her through the foyer, past a curving staircase and into a large family room. Beyond, through glass doors, she saw a pool landscaped with rocks and ferns, and splashed by a waterfall. Beside it, a dining and lounging area surrounded an outdoor kitchen.

"What a beautiful house." Jan didn't feel more than the tiniest prick of envy, though. She'd never pictured herself living anywhere so luxurious.

"Thanks. It was Tony's before we got married. I can still hardly believe I live here. Where's Kimmie?"

"Having lunch with a friend." Not exactly a lie.

Kate led the way into a sleek, upscale kitchen. "In the interest of world peace I sent Brady to his room."

"I hope he isn't being punished." Jan suspected Berry's mood was unrelated to anything the little boy had done.

"It's no punishment. I'm afraid he's a little spoiled with electronics, although we do limit his time on them."

Off the kitchen, in a sunroom with a bay window, a girl glanced up from the padded bench where she sat reading a fashion magazine. Although tall for a third-grader, Berry still had a childishly round face.

"Berry, this is Kimmie's mother, Mrs. Garcia," Kate said. "Or have you two met?"

"We have now," Jan said. As she registered the tightening of Berry's jaw, she wished Kate had introduced her differently, perhaps as a coworker of Zack's. But why should she? Kate had no idea how touchy this situation was for them. "I'm going to give you a ride. Hope that's okay."

The little girl stared at her, frowning, as if she'd like to refuse. "You can take the magazine," Kate offered. "I'm done with it."

Berry swung to her feet. "Thank you, Mrs. Franco." She held tightly to the publication with its cover image of a striking model. Although Jan disapproved of emphasizing thinness and sex appeal, she wouldn't mind if Kimmie showed more interest in wearing dresses once in a while.

"Don't forget your things." Kate pointed at a backpack. "How about I send you both home with some brownies?" To Jan, she explained, "I baked a double batch. We've got plenty."

"Daddy doesn't like me to eat sweets." Berry grabbed her pack.

Ordinarily, Jan would have accepted on Kimmie's behalf. But if Zack was strict about diet, she didn't want to make Berry feel bad. "It's kind of you, but Kimmie's been eating too many sweets herself." *Such as waffles for lunch.*

"I understand. Tony can always take them to work tomorrow."

In the car, Berry put on her seat belt and sat as far away from Jan as she could. Jan didn't blame her. Having Zack take another little girl to lunch was bad enough, and now she had to ride home with that girl's mom.

"The September issue is always the best." Jan indicated the splashy magazine in Berry's lap. "They feature the college back-to-school fashions. It's fun to see what's in style, isn't it?"

The girl flicked a sideways glance at her. "You read this?"

"I subscribe." Jan hadn't missed the fact Berry wore embroidered jeans and a white T-shirt with a rainbow on the front. Even in Southern California that seemed a bit casual for church and a performance. "Those are pretty colors you're wearing."

"I like dresses better." Berry stuck out her legs, which drew Jan's attention to her pink tennis shoes.

"Those are nice."

"They're ugly."

"You'd rather have patent-leather Mary Janes?" That was what Kimmie wore when she dressed up.

"What're those?"

Clearly Zack had a knowledge gap when it came to girls' clothes. "They're shiny and black with a strap across the top."

"I'd like that!"

Navigating away from the bluffs, Jan realized she hadn't considered logistics when she'd promised to take Berry home. She had a carful of groceries and her apartment was on the way.

The prospect of unthawed vegetables and hamburger patties won out. Also, she wasn't sure if Zack was home yet. "I have groceries in the trunk. I'd like to stop and put them in my fridge. Is that okay?"

Berry thought for a moment. "Yeah. Okay."

After the grandeur of the Franco house, arriving at her apartment complex made Jan more aware than ever of its modest stucco exterior, close-packed buildings and narrow walkways. Also, their carport was a hike from her unit, and she'd bought more groceries than she intended.

"I can carry some," Berry volunteered as Jan extracted her reusable bags from the cooler.

"That would be a big help." Jan settled a sack of frozen food into the girl's outstretched arms. She was able to carry the remaining groceries, and Berry fell into step beside her. They hauled their load past a pair of children running around shrieking in fun.

"You live here?" Berry asked.

"Sure do."

"Wow. Right next to the playground."

And here she'd been envying Zack's large yard! "You have a playhouse," Jan reminded her as they entered her apartment.

"It's no fun by myself."

Inside, the furniture seemed shabbier than ever. Well, it would look better when she brought in the new cushions, Jan decided. "Make yourself comfortable while I put the groceries away."

"Okay."

In the kitchen, Jan realized that she didn't usually give a ride to someone else's child without permission, let alone bring her home. She wondered if she'd overstepped. On the other hand, Zack was taking Kimmie to see his house and the kitten. Why shouldn't Berry get to know this place, too?

For better or worse, their lives were now entwined. Although Jan would never presume to think she could be like a mother to Berry, the girl needed a woman's guidance. A friend—like a big sister or aunt.

There wasn't much of a maternal influence in the child's life judging by what Zack had said. As for his mother, Elspeth Sargent rarely spoke up around her husband when Jan had known her. A sweet lady, but so self-effacing she practically disappeared.

In the other room, Berry put down the magazine. "May I use the bathroom?" she asked.

"Sure. Right through there." Jan pointed toward the hallway.

It took some rejuggling to fit everything into the freezer. She kept forgetting the small size of the apartment refrigerator. She'd have to shift her buying habits to more fresh, dried and canned food while they lived here.

With everything stowed, Jan noted the time. Two-thirty. Zack had estimated arriving here at three. If she drove Berry home now, they might miss each other. Besides, now that she thought about it, neither little girl was old enough to be left alone.

The girl hadn't returned from the bathroom. Jan found her in Kimmie's room standing in front of the canopy bed. From an overhead ruffle, pink drapes swept gracefully to tie-backs, revealing a white-and-pink quilt decorated with fairies. Berry turned slowly, taking in the princess-framed mirror with its crown points and the pink dresser topped by a tasseled lamp.

"It's like a fairy tale," Berry whispered.

To mention that Kimmie had lost all interest in princesses would only rub salt into the wound, Jan suspected. "Which fairy tale is your favorite?"

"Cinderella," Berry said at once. "She lost her mommy, too."

Jan had never considered the story from that angle. "That's true. But her daddy didn't take care of her the way yours does."

Her words flew right past the child. Kimmie had left the closet door ajar, and Berry was studying its colorful contents. "All those dresses!"

"I like them better than my daughter does," Jan admitted.

Longing shone in Berry's eyes as she tore herself away. "She's lucky to have a mommy, and now she has a daddy, too."

Telling an eight-year-old life wasn't always fair struck Jan as cruel. Luckily a better response popped into her head. "She doesn't have a kitten, though. We aren't allowed to keep pets in an apartment."

"You should buy a house," Berry said.

"I wish we could." No sense going into details. "Why don't we look through some other fashion magazines until your daddy gets here? He should be back soon."

"You have other fashion magazines?" That idea effectively distracted Berry.

"They're in my bedroom. Just a sec." Jan retrieved a couple, and she and Berry went to sit on the living-room couch. The little girl studied each picture eagerly, commenting on details that had escaped Jan's notice.

A short while later she heard Kimmie's excited voice outside, talking a mile a minute. "Those are the Mendez twins. They're always falling off the slide. Hi, Juan! Hi, Juanita! This is my dad." Obviously, she'd enjoyed their lunch.

Beside Jan, Berry froze. Well, the girls had to meet sometime, Jan reflected. But she'd have preferred not to spring it as a surprise on Zack.

WHEN HE'D USHERED KIMMIE into his house, Zack had wondered how she might react to seeing where he and Berry lived. On their tour of the first floor, she'd gazed wordlessly from the big-screen TV to the playhouse in the backyard, and he feared they might be reverting to an uncomfortable silence.

Then she said the magic words: "Where's Smidge?"

Upstairs, he opened the door to the bathroom. He'd installed a comfy cat bed, a variety of squeaky toys and a small climbing tree—not bad for a few days' work.

"Smidge! Wow, she's grown already." Kneeling, Kimmie allowed the kitten to sniff her before picking it up.

A warning about getting cat fur on her dress died unspoken. Despite the napkin, flecks of milk and chocolate had sneaked onto the pretty yellow fabric, and besides, Zack doubted Kimmie would care.

While she cuddled the kitten his thoughts wandered to Berry. How had her concert gone? Zack hoped she was enjoying Brady's company. With luck she'd forgotten about his date with Kimmie. Still, he didn't want to leave her at Kate's for too long, so after a few minutes he suggested they leave.

Now Kimmie skipped ahead of him along the walkway to her apartment. At last they were on the home stretch. Although Jan might object to her daughter's soiled clothes, Zack suspected the little girl would rumple almost anything she wore.

Kimmie banged on the door. When Jan opened it, the little girl said, "Hey, Mom! Guess what! Smidge is bigger already." Her body stiffened. "What's *she* doing here?"

Peering past her Zack felt a jolt of confusion. Why was Berry here? "What's going on?"

"I'll explain in a minute." Jan ushered them inside.

The girls glared at each other. "You took her to our

house?" Berry demanded. "You let her play with my kitten?"

Zack was framing a response when Kimmie leaped into the fray. "I found him first! And what are you doing here? My mom isn't *your* mommy."

"Well, my daddy isn't…" Berry broke off.

"Yes, he is!" Kimmie said triumphantly. "And we had waffles for lunch."

"You let her eat waffles?" Berry fixed accusing eyes on Zack.

"For a special occasion." No telling how Jan had pulled it off, but she'd undercut his lunch with Kimmie. He'd trusted her, and now this?

"You didn't let her play with my toys, did you?" Berry demanded.

"Only the kitten," he said tightly. They'd sort this out later when they were alone.

"Girls, you're both cranky," Jan said. "Your dad and I need to talk in private."

"She can't come in my room," Kimmie shot back.

"Fine. You go change clothes and be sure to put stain stick on those spots. Berry, would you mind taking these magazines into my bedroom and reading them there?" Expertly, Jan shepherded the children to separate spaces.

Zack barely hung on to his temper. It didn't help to see his daughter clutching a publication with a cover model who wore outrageous makeup and a skimpy, clingy blouse. He'd seen girls at the elementary school in such trashy fashions and, while Jan dressed her own daughter modestly, he didn't want Berry getting the wrong idea.

Not that there was anything wrong with Jan's sense of style. Wrapped in a cloud of soft pink, she seemed luminous. Maybe that had something to do with her maternal instincts.

*Stay focused.* "What were you thinking?" he demanded once the bedroom doors were safely closed. "I can't believe you picked her up and brought her here without my permission."

Fishing in her pocket, she produced his cell phone. "You left this."

Okay, he'd made a mistake. That didn't justify Jan's actions. "You should have brought it to the restaurant. I might have had an important call."

"I was monitoring it." Jan took a guarded stance with chin raised. She looked small and defiant, much like her daughter. "I didn't want to interrupt you and Kimmie."

"That wasn't your decision."

"Whose decision was it?" she retorted. "Furthermore, it was probably a good thing I took the call. Berry and Brady were squabbling. Kate needed someone to pick her up. That would have ruined your lunch for sure."

"You answered my phone." Zack ran an agitated hand through his hair. He disliked quarreling. What was it about Jan that broke through his usual reserve? "It could have been the hospital. Did it occur to you what people might think? What did you tell Kate?"

"That we had a mix-up with the phones," she responded coolly. "It's almost impossible to keep secrets in a hospital for long, anyway, especially since you told people we used to be engaged."

"You're going to drag that into the discussion?" he snapped.

A small noise drew Zack's attention to the hallway. Clutching a stuffed bear, Kimmie regarded them in dismay. "You're fighting like Allie's parents."

"That was her best friend in Houston," Jan explained. "Her parents got divorced."

Mother and daughter stood in almost the same attitude,

heads cocked and foreheads puckered. A matched set except for the little girl's blazing green eyes.

"I didn't realize the walls were so thin," Zack told Kimmie. "We aren't really fighting."

"Yes, you are," she answered. "Tell the truth."

He blinked, taken aback. Berry would never speak to him that way. *Watch out. What you say now could overshadow everything else today.* "You're right. We're arguing."

"You and Berry were arguing, too," Jan told the little girl. "Sometimes people lose their tempers. Then they get over it."

"Are you over it?" she asked her mom.

"I hope so." Jan stared at Zack as if daring him to disagree.

She had some nerve to consider him in the wrong! Still, he was the one who'd forgotten his phone, Zack conceded. And if he'd taken Kate's call, it would indeed have disrupted his lunch with Kimmie.

"We need to finish our discussion," he told the child as gently as he could. "We'll try to keep our voices down."

Her mother nodded. "Back to your room, sweetie."

Hugging her bear, the little girl trudged off. Zack waited until he heard the door shut. "Like it or not, we have to coordinate our parenting," he muttered.

"I did my best to respect your wishes. Kate offered us brownies to take home. When Berry said you didn't allow it, I declined for Kimmie also." Jan remained standing. "I'm not the enemy here."

"I realize that." Might as well get another issue off his chest. "You had no way of knowing, but in future I'd rather Berry didn't read fashion magazines. Children ought to dress like children."

"I think I dress Kimmie just fine," she scoffed.

Did she have to take everything as an insult? "I didn't mean it that way. Kimmie looks cute."

"Adult fashions aren't suitable for children," Jan admitted in turn. "But..."

"If Berry goes around in frilly clothes she'll avoid exercising." That was the heart of the matter. Literally. "I don't want her afraid to get her clothes dirty."

"That doesn't seem to stop Kimmie," Jan said wryly. A tiny smile lit her face. "Besides, Berry was reading one of those magazines at Kate's. I wish Kimmie took as much interest in girlie stuff as Berry does."

"Kimmie seems more resilient than my..." He'd been about to say "my daughter," but that term applied to both girls. "Than Berry."

Jan glanced toward the hallway. "Seeing how upset they both are, I suggest we postpone further contact for a few weeks."

Was that her agenda? "Don't think for a minute I'll back off. I'm Kimmie's father."

"Did you hear me denying it?" Jan protested. "I didn't have to take this appointment at Safe Harbor. I could have kept Kimmie away from you forever. I chose not to do that."

Despite his fighting instincts, Zack backed off. "Fine. We'll wait a week or so before setting another appointment. By then, maybe Berry won't feel so threatened." Also, he was on call at the hospital the following Saturday, and he and Berry planned to attend a wedding next Sunday.

"Okay. If there's anything I can do for her..."

"For Berry? She's great." He'd put a lot of effort into building a safe environment for his daughter, with sitters he trusted and regular visits to his parents and her uncle. Plus a lot of one-on-one time with him.

"I'll see you at work, then," Jan said.

"Right." Thank goodness for that neutral, professional setting. There, Jan was less likely to be impulsive and Zack could more easily control his temper. With time, they should be able to establish a balanced relationship.

Satisfied for the moment, he went to get Berry.

## Chapter Nine

The next week Jan held sessions with small groups of staffers to discuss the egg bank's protocols. At school, Kimmie settled in, making new friends and, as far as Jan could determine, avoiding Berry. Thank goodness the girls were a year apart.

The second week, at Zack's suggestion, she attended a Tuesday support group of fertility patients, inviting their input and getting a sense of their concerns.

Zack stayed in the background, while a psychologist encouraged the women—and a few husbands—to speak up. Their concerns about egg donations, Jan learned, centered on legal issues. Since the laws in California differed from those in Texas, she couldn't give specific answers but assured them she was working with the hospital attorney to make sure parents didn't risk having a donor show up later, demanding rights to the child.

"I'll get back to you with more details," she promised. Immediately afterward she put in a call to Tony Franco and set up a meeting for his first available slot. She'd intended to do that, anyway.

"Going to the support group was a good idea, Dr. Sargent," she told Zack, aware that others might overhear as they walked along the hall toward her office. "I learned a lot."

A nurse headed in the opposite direction glanced at Zack appreciatively. He *was* striking, with his emerald gaze and slightly mussed hair inviting a woman to stroke it into place. Jan's fingers twitched instinctively.

"You have a talent for working with groups." He gave no indication he noticed the nurse. "They feel comfortable with you."

The praise warmed Jan. "Thanks."

"How's…" He broke off as several people walked by.

Seeking an update on Kimmie, Jan guessed. She was curious to find out how Berry was doing, also. But they couldn't talk here.

"We do need to set something up," she told him as they neared the first-floor fertility suite. "I'll text you."

"It can be difficult to…" He stopped.

At her desk Caroline Carter swung away from her computer with an expression that struck Jan as a little too innocent. The secretary hit a key, closing a website, but not before Jan saw the familiar Twitter site.

"What's the hospital's policy about personal use of computers?" she demanded rhetorically.

"I'm so sorry." This wasn't the first time the young woman had been reprimanded for social networking on the job. And that was in addition to her gossiping in the cafeteria, Jan reflected. "One of my friends is having a baby and she's tweeting from the delivery room. Isn't that fascinating?"

"It's weird," Jan said.

"Not as unusual as you might assume," Zack responded.

"Your patients do that?" During Kimmie's birth, Jan had been caught up in the agony and then the joy. Besides, if she'd pulled a stunt like texting, her mother—

who'd served as her labor coach—would have snatched the phone out of her hand.

"A few."

"You don't object?"

"They're not supposed to use cell phones." Zack shrugged. "But it does take their minds off the pain."

"And pulls them out of the experience of their lives," Jan noted.

Caroline sat listening avidly. A pretty young woman in her twenties with skin a shade darker than Berry's and shoulder-length black hair, she'd worked for a while in Dr. Tartikoff's office. *A personality mismatch if there ever was one.*

In front of her, Jan didn't dare say another word about anything personal. "I have to go. Melissa Everhart and I are driving to the Rowland Hacienda Egg Bank. The director offered to discuss their program and share their protocols with us." The location was about an hour's drive inland.

"They don't see us as competition?" Zack asked. "I should think they'd be careful how much information they share."

"We won't compete for donors, since most of their clientele is Asian." A large Chinese community lived in the east L.A. County area. "Also, don't forget that egg banks cooperate when recipients request hard-to-find blood types and genetic backgrounds. The more donors we identify, the better we can all serve our clients."

"Oh!" Caroline gave a start. "I meant to tell you. Melissa went home sick. She said she must have eaten a bad breakfast burrito."

"Is she all right?" The IVF coordinator was single, and Jan couldn't recall whether she lived alone. "I should check on her."

"One of the volunteers, Renée Green, drove her home and offered to stay with her awhile," Caroline said. "Do you want me to call and see how she's doing?"

"Yes, please." What a disappointment. Jan had looked forward to touring the facility with Melissa and sharing her input afterward. Having a second set of trained eyes and ears was invaluable. "I wish I could postpone the visit, but I can't do that at the last minute."

"I have a light schedule on Tuesday afternoons," Zack said. "I'll come with you."

*Caroline will inform the entire hospital within five minutes.* Refusing his offer would only invite further speculation, though.

"That would be helpful. As a physician, you'll have insights into areas beyond my expertise." Annoyed by the receptionist's answering smirk, Jan addressed her sternly. "Caroline, I'm going to start following you on Twitter. If I see any messages during work hours, or anything ever in a public forum that pertains to hospital personnel, I will report it to Dr. Rayburn."

"I won't. I promise." The young woman looked suitably chastened. That ought to last for what, half an hour? And it wouldn't stop her from yakking to her fellow gossips on staff.

Well, no sense making anything more of this. Jan needed to get on the road soon to keep her appointment. And despite the awkwardness, she'd meant what she said about valuing Zack's observations.

He was on the phone with his nurse, saying, "Good, good." No problems with his schedule, it appeared.

The trip would also give them a chance to set his next "date" with Kimmie. Beyond that, the two of them got along best when they kept things strictly professional. Just what Jan intended to do.

RIDING ON THE PASSENGER side of Jan's sedan, Zack sneaked a glance at her profile—at the shapely nose and expressive face even as she concentrated on the freeway traffic. It surprised him how powerfully he felt connected to her despite the pain they'd inflicted on each other.

When he'd learned Jan had kept their daughter, Zack had been determined to make up for lost time. Realistically, he knew that couldn't happen overnight, but his sense of justice had demanded compensation for the years he'd lost with Kimmie.

Things were more complicated than he'd expected.

He liked Jan, and her input about Berry was valuable. The situation with Kimmie troubled his older daughter more than he'd anticipated. Having been his first priority since her toddler years, she should feel secure in his love, yet his lunch with Kimmie had upset Berry. The effects persisted despite his efforts to restore a sense of normalcy.

Jan must have been thinking along the same lines. She broke the silence by asking, "How's Berry?"

"Fine," he answered automatically.

She slanted a skeptical look at him. "None of my business, right?"

Perhaps. Yet he needed to talk to someone. After Rima's death Zack had taken Berry to counseling, which had helped them both. In the three years since, he'd relied on occasional conversations with teachers and sitters to fill in the gaps of his own awareness. He'd never faced anything like the changes he saw in her now, however.

Too bad his own parents weren't a resource. He simply didn't have that kind of trusting relationship with them.

"Okay, she's not fine. She's grumpy and spends a lot of time in her room with the kitten," he said. "And there are other things. I'm not sure how much is because of me having another daughter and how much is simply because she's getting older."

"What things?" Jan prompted.

"Saturday night, while I was on call, she slept at her sitter's house," Zack recalled. "She usually enjoys that, but when I picked her up Sunday she complained about having to share a room with their sixteen-month-old. Until now, she's always enjoyed playing with Rachel."

"I suspect she felt uneasy about being away from you." Jan changed lanes to bypass a line of slowing vehicles.

"Probably." He'd have liked to stop there because the other incident that sprang to mind was embarrassing. But he'd appreciate the feedback. "On Sunday, we were invited to a wedding. You know Paige Brennan?" He and Paige had formed a friendship because both were relatively new at the hospital. Also, learning advanced surgical techniques from Dr. Tartikoff had thrown them together.

"I've met her," Jan acknowledged. "She's Erica's obstetrician, and Erica likes her a lot."

"Well, Berry was excited about going. Then she put on her best dress and it was very short." Zack's heart had gone out to his clearly distressed little girl. "Her shoes were too small, as well. It hadn't occurred to me to take her shopping, and by then it was too late. She wore tights and we made the best of it."

"Kids grow fast," Jan replied, as she navigated toward the ramp connecting to another freeway. "I'm sure no one noticed."

"No one except Berry." *But she was the one who counted.*

"How was the wedding?"

"Beautiful, not that I'm any expert." Held in a chapel overlooking the harbor, the small ceremony had been packed with coworkers and the couple's family. Paige had two sisters and three brothers, while the groom, detective Mike Aaron, also came from a large family. "Afterwards, Berry asked about Rima's and my wedding. She wondered why we don't have any pictures."

"Why don't you?"

"We got married at the county courthouse with my parents as witnesses." Zack wished they'd made Berry a flower girl. What a memorable photo that would have been! But she'd been a toddler at the time, too young to care about such things, and he hadn't thought about the future.

Jan frowned. "Nobody took pictures?"

"My dad shot a couple that came out so blurry he didn't save them." Later, when Zack apologized for not hiring a photographer, Rima had shrugged it off. They'd have plenty of chances to take photos, she'd said. But they couldn't recapture their wedding.

"How did Berry react when you explained?"

"She didn't say anything." Zack sighed. "I used to think she had a remarkably calm attitude about things. I'm beginning to realize she simply hides her emotions well."

"Kimmie's very open, which isn't always a blessing," Jan remarked.

"Has she been acting out?" Zack wondered if postponing their next outing had been a mistake. "Is she upset we didn't go out last weekend?"

Busy watching the traffic, Jan didn't respond. Zack was about to repeat the question, when he noticed her lips clamped together.

"She has been, hasn't she?" he prodded.

"I'm an idiot." Jan shot him a quick glance. "What did I imagine was going to happen when we came back to this area? I figured you were married with kids, and you'd stay out of the picture. Stupid, stupid, stupid."

"You're upset because I want a relationship with my daughter?" That irked him. "I'd be a poor excuse for a father if I didn't."

"You took no interest in her seven years ago!" she accused. "No, wait. Stop. Forget I said that, okay?"

He choked back the angry words threatening to overflow his self-control. "I'll try."

"It was uncalled for," Jan agreed. "I have no idea how she feels about you *or* me. She's deflecting all her emotions on to the cat business."

"Cat business?"

"She keeps harping on how unfair it is that Berry gets to keep Smidge." Jan's voice frayed.

"It is a little unfair, I suppose," Zack conceded.

"Now she's feeding that stray cat she calls Gorilla." Jan sucked in a breath. "I've been looking at ads for apartments but the only ones that accept pets charge higher rent and insist on a large deposit." She indicated a piece of paper he'd shifted aside when he sat down. "Now she's nagging to go to that."

The flyer advertised a pet-adoption fair at the Oahu Lane Shelter on the following Saturday. "Where'd this come from?"

"School." The car slowed as it entered an off-ramp for Rowland Heights. "If I take her, she'll only press harder to adopt a kitten."

"What if I take her?" He'd been looking for an event that might interest Kimmie.

"You don't mind?"

"Why should I?" Kimmie could hardly nag him, since he had no say in whether she got a cat.

"She'll be thrilled. You're already a hero for rescuing Smidge." Jan's voice quavered. "I wish…"

"What?" Zack asked.

"I wish I weren't coming off as the bad guy."

He hadn't meant to put her in that light. "Jan, I may resent the way you've acted—I do resent it—but I have no intention of undercutting you with Kimmie. That would be unfair to both of you."

She stopped at a red light. "It's scary for me. Daddies mean a lot to little girls, especially since she's never had one."

Jan was afraid of losing her daughter's love? Irrational, but understandable, too. "Just because she loves her dad doesn't mean she's going to abandon her mom. That'll never happen."

"I suppose not." She swallowed. "She needs both."

Wistfully, he added, "So does Berry. I do my best."

"You've been wonderful with her. She's such a sweetie."

They entered the lot of a large medical building. "Berry's invited to her best friend's birthday party on Saturday," Zack said. "While she's gone, I can take Kimmie to the fair."

"Berry won't mind missing the event? She might want to go, too." Jan seemed genuinely concerned about his stepdaughter.

"I'll explain beforehand." Zack had learned the more kids knew the score in advance, the better things went. "I'll point out that Kimmie just gets to see the cats, while Berry can keep Smidge."

"Good idea." Jan parked between an SUV and a sports car. "Don't forget to take Berry clothes shopping before the party."

"Thanks for the reminder." Zack had no idea what little girls wore to birthday parties these days, but no doubt the saleslady could help.

As he reached for the door, a light touch on his arm halted him. "We don't have to be at odds, Zack."

"I never said we were," he replied, puzzled.

"Let me rephrase that. We both have a lot to gain by working together, for the girls' sake." Up close, Jan's dark eyes were mesmerizing. The softness of her hair and scent of flowers made Zack keenly aware of how much he missed this woman. If her mouth were a few inches closer, he might not be able to stop his lips from descending on hers.

A sharply drawn breath indicated her reaction. *If we could start over, if this were fresh and new...*

But it wasn't. And they couldn't.

Jan drew back. "They're waiting for us inside."

"Right." His throat tight, Zack pushed the door handle. After the chasm they'd created between them, the best they could hope for now was to cooperate and respect each other. On Saturday, he would take Kimmie to the adoption fair. After that, they'd set up a schedule of regular visits.

Having a predictable system ought to help Berry adjust—and Zack, as well.

DURING THE NEXT FEW days, the moment when she'd nearly kissed Zack replayed through Jan's thoughts. They'd both felt the same magnetic pull, the same longings.

What if they hadn't resisted? Where could it lead?

Over the years she'd wondered what their lives might have been like if not for that incompetent doctor and the lying supervisor at their old hospital. But the real problem was Zack had stood against her instead of giving her the benefit of the doubt.

Still, Jan was glad he'd accompanied her to the egg bank. On the drive home, he'd made useful observations about the facility's procedures, recruitment techniques and counseling services. What a twist of fate that of all the doctors at Safe Harbor, he took the keenest interest in the egg-donor program.

Later in the week Jan met with the Safe Harbor attorney to discuss the rights of egg donors and recipients. Kate's husband, a thoughtful man in his mid-thirties, welcomed her into his large office and answered her questions with care.

"In the early days, the field of egg donation used to be the Wild West—unregulated territory," Tony explained from behind his broad desk. "So did surrogate motherhood and other fertility practices. Since then, laws and court rulings have gone a long way toward spelling out all parties' rights and obligations."

Jan already knew the donor had to sign a contract agreeing to undergo medical and psychological screening, as well as genetic testing. The contract specified that the egg recipient and father of the child became the legal parents.

"In addition, in California, both the egg recipient and the father, once they've signed documents, have legal obligations regarding the child regardless of whether they're genetically related to it," Tony continued. "The egg donor is protected, too. For example, just as with a sperm donor, she can't be sued for child support."

"The prospective parents want to be certain no one can come after them and take their child away." Knowing how she'd worried about the possibility of Zack claiming rights to Kimmie, Jan empathized.

"That issue arose in the UCI scandal," Tony replied. Behind him, through a large window, Jan caught a distant glimmer of the ocean. "In that instance the genetic mothers hadn't agreed to give up their eggs."

"What happened?" She'd heard a lot about the case, but not the individual outcomes.

"By the time the scandal broke, many of the children were toddlers or nearing school age," Tony said. "Most of the unwilling donors understood the kids and the recipients were innocent victims, but it was heartbreaking. To the best of my knowledge, none of the children were removed from their homes. I believe in some cases the genetic parents were allowed limited contact."

Jan shuddered. "It must have been horrible for everyone."

"Which is why we will be very, very careful with our contracts and procedures," Tony said. "As I'm sure you agree."

"Absolutely."

After they went over other questions raised by the support group, Jan left his office with extensive notes and Tony's promise to attend the next meeting with her. And, of course, for the two of them to consult further as he drew up the contracts.

All might be well on the work front, but at home, Kimmie continued to sneak food to the cat. By now, it seemed highly unlikely Gorilla had an owner.

"Do you want to take him to the shelter tomorrow so he can find a home?" Jan asked her daughter on Friday.

"No!" Kimmie glared at her. "They'll kill him."

"They don't do that."

"He'd hate it," the little girl insisted. "I won't let you!"

Since she, too, disliked the idea of handing over the cat, Jan dropped the subject. On Saturday morning, however, she wished she hadn't.

## Chapter Ten

At four-thirty in the morning the yowling of tomcats awakened Jan. Grumpily, she pulled the pillow over her head.

Over the next half-hour random noises disturbed her sleep. Worn-out from an intense week, she barely broke the surface of awareness.

Then a series of screeches vibrated through her head, so loud they might have originated in the next room. Startled and annoyed, she shot out of bed. She'd closed her window last night, so why was she hearing...

"Stop it! Stop it now!" Kimmie screamed.

Without bothering with slippers or robe, Jan bolted across the room and flung open the door.

Two furry shapes flew around her living room, their squalling punctuated by a sharp, offensive odor. Cowering in a corner, Kimmie waved her hands uselessly at a pair of battling tomcats.

"What on earth?" As she stepped into the room Jan's first thought was to protect her daughter. "Kimmie, stay back."

"The bad cat chased Gorilla in here! He's hurting him."

The front door stood wide-open. As she registered that fact, Jan realized the landlord couldn't fail to notice this disturbance directly beneath him. Well, she'd deal with him later. Right now she had to focus on getting these crazed cats out of her apartment.

A large gray-and-white creature barely recognizable as Gorilla raced by, pursued by an even bigger black cat with a brown patch over its nose. They became a furious ball atop her sofa. One of them caught a claw in the fabric then ripped it free, leaving a gash with stuffing poking out. Shaky with shock, Jan ran to the closet and grabbed a broom.

"Don't hurt Gorilla!" Kimmie cried.

"Go in your room and close the door," Jan commanded. "There's no telling how they're going to react. I don't want you injured."

"But, Mom!"

"Do you want your clothes and toys ruined, too? Go, and shut the door tight!"

Her daughter obeyed tearfully.

Jan hated seeing Kimmie upset, although she supposed there was a good lesson here. If her daughter had followed the rules this wouldn't have happened. As for the cats, she aimed her fury at the irresponsible people who'd left them to battle over territory.

A few whacks of the broom failed to connect with the fast-moving animals, but the near misses sent them skittering out the doorway. A few more screeches and they were gone.

Leaning on the broom, Jan gazed in dismay at the slashed upholstery. An acrid smell permeated everything. How could two small animals cause so much damage in such a short time?

The descending staircase thudded with the angry stomp of masculine footsteps. As if things weren't bad enough, here came the landlord.

AT ELEVEN O'CLOCK, AFTER dropping Berry at her friend's party, Zack arrived to find Jan's door standing open. Inside, the scent of lemon cleaner failed to mask an unpleasant animal odor.

As he knocked on the frame, he saw that furniture had been shoved to one side and cushions piled by the door. What had happened here?

A frazzled Jan hurried toward him. In stark contrast to her usual careful grooming, she'd tied her hair crookedly in a ponytail and wore an oversize T-shirt.

"Cat fight," she said before he could ask, and heaved a couple of deep breaths. "Oh, Zack…"

"Tell me." As he entered, he resisted an urge to put his arms around her. "Is Kimmie okay?"

"Yes. She's in her room, which is one of the few places still intact." Her hands fluttered in agitation as she described how the little girl had tried to rescue Gorilla and instead allowed a pair of furious tomcats to trash their living room. "As if that weren't bad enough, the landlord's throwing us out. Immediately."

"He can't. It isn't even your cat."

"He says we violated our lease. Kimmie *was* bringing the cat inside."

About to suggest they fight the eviction, Zack realized it might be more trouble and expense than the apartment was worth. "He has to give you thirty days' notice."

"Maybe, but that doesn't change the fact that this place is unsanitary." Jan indicated the stained carpet in disgust. "I've done my best to clean up so we can spend a few nights in our rooms, but Mr. Withers says the walls have to be repainted and the carpets cleaned or possibly replaced. According to him, it may cost several thousand dollars and I'm responsible."

If the landlord had to replace the carpet, that *would*

be steep. "Since you're paying, why can't you move back in afterward?"

"He wants us gone." Jan's shoulders sagged. "He said he'd pay half the cost if we move out within three days."

"And that's okay with you?" Zack was willing to help her fight this if she needed more time.

Another sigh. "Half the cost could be significant."

"Be sure he gives you itemized receipts."

"I will." Jan sounded uncharacteristically defeated. "I was just getting the place fixed up and now I have to find a new one."

Surely Safe Harbor had vacancies. "That shouldn't be too difficult."

"As long as we're moving, we need a place that allows pets," she said.

"You're sure about that?" Zack eyed the ruined cushions.

"If Kimmie had her own cat, she wouldn't be collecting strays."

To him that bordered on rewarding the girl for breaking rules. Still, he'd seen enough strong-willed behavior from Berry recently to understand the value of compromise.

"My mom says we can stay with her for a while," Jan continued. "I won't have to find storage, since a lot of the furniture has to be thrown out and we can pile the rest in her garage. But her dog hates cats, so it's goodbye, Gorilla. Not that I have any idea where he is."

"Need help moving?" Zack sometimes assisted friends from church. A pickup truck, a few strong backs and a couple of trips usually sufficed.

"That's very kind, but unnecessary." She stretched her neck, which must be cramped from the cleaning. Zack wished he could run his hands across her sore muscles, massaging the knots and relieving her tension. "I've hired a moving van for Monday evening. We'll pack tomorrow. Good thing I saved our cardboard boxes in the carport storage space."

Zack admired her efficiency, as well as her calm response to this crisis. Well, he had only a few hours before picking up Berry. "I should get Kimmie. Is she under any punishment I should know about?"

"I suppose…" She blinked away whatever she'd started to say. "No, having to move and give up her cat seems hard enough. I think she's learned a lesson. That's the point of punishment, isn't it?"

Zack had never thought of it, but then, he'd raised such a compliant child that discipline was rarely required. "I suppose it is."

"I'll get her." Jan vanished into the hall.

Zack wondered how he would react to an incident like this. His instincts called for serious repercussions, but how much was enough?

A long-ago episode popped into his mind. At six or seven, Zack had used permanent markers that bled through the paper onto an unprotected table. The memory of the spanking stung, but even worse was his father's rage. His dad had confiscated the money Zack had saved from Christmas gifts to help pay for refinishing.

After that, Zack had taken great care with the furniture. He'd also begun to mistrust his father emotionally. The lesson he'd learned from an overly harsh penalty had gone far beyond the one his father intended.

A moment later, the sight of Kimmie's tear-streaked face showed she was already suffering consequences. "You might want to wash up before we go," Zack said gently. "So we don't make the animals sad."

"Oh!" She raised a hand to her damp cheek. "Okay." And hurried to the bathroom.

"You're good with her," Jan said quietly.

*So are you.* But he couldn't bring himself to say the words aloud.

Water splashed, and a moment later Kimmie emerged, ready to go. Zack turned to Jan. "We'll see you later."

"Enjoy the animals. I'll be searching the internet for a new place."

He left with his daughter skipping ahead. Between two buildings, Zack thought he spotted a gray-and-white feline peering at them wistfully, but when he looked again, it was gone.

THE OAHU LANE SHELTER occupied a rambling building in a complex that included several auto-repair shops. Zack and Kimmie joined a stream of patrons passing below a Pet Adoption Day banner and into the facility. Excited barking and some anxious mewing drifted from the interior.

A wall sign advertised low-cost spay and neuter services, as well as microchipping to recover lost pets. "We could get Gorilla fixed here," Zack said. "This might be a good place to bring Smidge, too."

He and Berry had read on a website that it was important to get her spayed by the age of six months. He wished he knew exactly how old she was—he made a mental note to take her to a vet soon to learn her age and get her shots.

"Okay." Kimmie scuffed the cement floor with her tennis shoes.

Zack didn't push her to show enthusiasm for their visit. Instead, he asked, "You worried about moving?"

"We have to stay with Grandma and Wiener hates cats." That must be the dog.

"I see."

"Please sign in over here." A freckled teenage boy directed them to a clipboard on the front counter. "Are you looking for any specific type of animal?"

"We like cats," Zack answered as he got in line to register.

"There's a twenty-five percent discount on adoption fees today. That includes spay-neuter and microchipping," he said. "We'll be starting a tour soon."

"Great. Thanks."

A short while later a young woman came to guide them. When Zack inquired about the spay-neuter program, she informed him the surgeries were performed at a regional center with volunteer veterinarians. "We just house them here temporarily and transport them."

"That's a good service."

"We do the best we can on a shoestring."

Kimmie brightened at the sight of cages full of cats. "They're so cute! How can people give them up?"

Zack didn't have an answer. He hadn't intended to adopt Smidge, but already she'd become part of the family.

While Kimmie oohed and aahed over a bunch of fluffy kittens, he saw a few of his patients among the visitors. They greeted him warmly and said hello to his daughter. None of them had met Berry, so he was spared from making explanations.

Zack also recognized one of his neighbors, an energetic woman in her seventies whom he often saw walking her dogs. She wore the blue blazer that served as a uniform for shelter employees. "You work here?" he said.

She thrust out her hand and they shook. "I'm Ilsa Ivy."

"I'm Zack Sargent, and this is Kimmie." He noted her name tag. "You're the director."

"That's me."

"You get to play with animals every day?" Kimmie asked in awe.

Ilsa chuckled. "I wish I had time to do more of that. Mostly I'm busy fund-raising." She indicated a sign proclaiming a campaign to upgrade the facilities. "Thanks to adoption fees and people's generosity, we're able to meet our operating expenses. Unfortunately, our plumbing and air-conditioning systems need replacing to the tune of twenty thousand dollars. Otherwise the city is threatening to pull our permit."

"I'll certainly make a donation." Zack reached for his wallet. "Do you take credit cards?"

"Yes, on our website," Ilsa responded, and gave him a card with the address. "We and the animals appreciate anything you can do." With a friendly nod she went off to speak to another family.

Zack tucked the card into his wallet. He'd make the donation today.

"Twenty thousand dollars is a lot of money," Kimmie said dejectedly.

"Yes, it is." His gift wouldn't go far, but he supposed every contribution helped. "Hungry?"

"Yes." His daughter appeared deep in thought as they crossed the parking lot. Abruptly, she said, "What if someone brings Gorilla here? They might run out of money and have to kill him."

"I don't think that's likely."

She gave a little hop. "I know how we can keep him!"

"How?" Zack beeped to unlock his car.

"We could move in with you!"

He supposed he should have seen that coming. Instead, he felt blindsided.

"Uh…" Zack replied.

"I THOUGHT I SHOULD explain." Zack's voice sent a tingle down Jan's spine.

Surprised by her instinctive reaction to him, she closed her computer file and swung her desk chair to face him. The fact that she left her office door open for visitors, combined with the usual midafternoon hospital bustle, must be the reason she hadn't heard his approach. Also the details of tonight's move kept tumbling through her brain.

The sight of his masculine body standing in the doorway provided a new distraction. "Explain what?"

"We didn't have a chance to talk when I brought her back on Saturday." Jan had been on the phone with a moving company. "Kimmie's probably explained that she suggested staying with me."

A lump formed in Jan's throat. "I wouldn't allow it. Not by herself." An irrational fear warned that, if forced to choose, the little girl might abandon her mom for daddy's big house.

*You're letting anxiety get the better of your judgment.* It had been clear from Kimmie's comments she assumed the two adults could get along as housemates.

"Both of you, of course." Zack thrust his hands into the pockets of his white coat. "And Gorilla, which I presume is the main point."

"I did hear about that." All evening and most of Sunday, her daughter had given Jan the hard sell. Taking no for an answer went against Kimmie's nature.

"She wasn't hurt that I said no, was she?" Zack went on. "She caught me off guard. I could have been more diplomatic."

"Oh?" Jan hadn't observed any signs of painful rejection in her daughter. Still, she *would* like to hear his side of the conversation. "What did you say?"

"I explained that my house is Berry's home. She lost her mom. Now she's found out I have another daughter, and it's hard for her." Zack blew out a short breath. "I didn't mean to use Berry as an excuse. The last thing I want is to create more antagonism between those two."

"Judging by her comments, you also mentioned the cats not getting along," Jan recalled.

"Right." He gave her a sideways grin. "I'm afraid I latched on to any argument that sprang to mind."

"You feeling guilty? You shouldn't." In Jan's opinion, moving in with Zack was not remotely feasible. Especially when he managed to be so appealing, with his green eyes glimmering apologetically.

"She did say…" A crease formed on his forehead. "'Why can't we live with you? You're supposed to be my daddy, but you act like you're just Berry's daddy.'"

"Ouch." Jan chuckled. "My daughter's much too good at guilt manipulation."

He grinned back. "You mean *our* daughter. I suppose I have to take my share of the blame."

"Big of you." She was laughing until she glimpsed movement behind him, just outside the office. *Uh-oh.*

Springing up, Jan ignored his puzzled expression as she rushed past him. In the outer office, Caroline Carter was settling herself behind her computer.

"What?" Zack swung around until Jan felt his warmth against her back.

They shouldn't stand here in full view, like a pair of lovers. Even if that's what they'd once been.

Half turning, she became keenly aware of his woodsy fragrance mixed with a trace of iodine-scented surgical scrub. Quickly, she put some distance between them. "Our secret is out."

"Excuse me?" He appeared unaware of the minefield they'd stepped in just now.

"Our secretary was eavesdropping." To be fair, she added, "Or she just happened to be in the right place at the wrong time for us."

"What could she have heard?"

Jan recalled the most important detail. "You used the words *our daughter.*"

Zack glanced out, frowning, and Jan followed his gaze. The young woman was on the phone. An innocuous conversation from what she could hear, but louder than necessary. *For our benefit, no doubt.*

"Any chance she missed it?" Zack asked.

"She peeled off at supersonic speed. It's lucky the boom didn't knock us over." Jan considered marching out and ordering Caroline to zip it. But on the far side of the reception area, Melissa's door stood wide-open and Karen's was also ajar. Plus Dr. Cole Rattigan's office was next to Jan's, within easy earshot. Openly rebuking the young woman would be like pouring oil on a fire. Warning her in private might keep the embers smoldering, though likely not for long.

"The best way to run damage control is to get ahead of the curve," Jan told Zack. "Given that some people already know we were engaged, we might as well tell them you're Kimmie's dad. The staff who knew me in Boston probably suspect it already."

"Too bad people don't mind their own business." His affable air shifted into coolness. "Still, you're right. If we're forthright, it'll take some of the sting out of the gossip."

"We don't have to make a big deal of it." Jan felt a touch of relief he'd agreed so readily.

"There'll be questions, spoken or unspoken. I'd rather we addressed them than left people to speculate."

Questions. Awkward ones. "I guess we have to tell them I kept Kimmie a secret all these years. It's going to make me look bad."

Although Zack might have relished payback, she saw no satisfaction on his face. "We should also tell them I signed the relinquishment paper. And I got engaged to another woman before Kimmie was born. No matter how I feel about what you did, that's between you and me."

If only he'd meet her gaze…but that was asking too much. "Thank you."

"We have to protect the girls. It was bound to come out sooner or later." Zack cast a disapproving glare in Caroline's direction. "I'm on a tight schedule. Catch you later."

"Later."

Jan wished they had more time to get their balance before going public. Well, they couldn't undo what was done.

If the metaphor hadn't been so painful, she'd have said the cat was out of the bag.

# Chapter Eleven

For the rest of Monday afternoon Jan passed the word along as casually as she could, aware the rumors might already have spread. "As you may have heard…" was how she phrased it to coworkers whose paths crossed hers.

"We all have our issues," was Erica's judicious response. The nurse had suffered through a painful divorce back in Boston. "Safe Harbor's a good place for second chances."

"I'm glad to hear it," Jan said. "How're you feeling these days?"

With the baby due in a month, Erica had given up assisting at surgeries. Too much standing, and her bump got in the way. Although she claimed to enjoy reviewing charts and handling other desk jobs, Jan knew her friend chafed at the restriction. "I ache all over. Thank goodness my husband gives great back rubs."

They parted with mutual warm wishes. *How wonderful to have a friend and ally here,* Jan thought.

Dr. Tartikoff, who'd been grumpier than usual without his favorite scrub nurse, managed a rare smile at Jan's confession. "Always wondered who the dad was. Glad he's stepping up to the plate."

"He's great with Kimmie," Jan said.

"Good." With a nod, the surgeon headed off.

Jan departed earlier than usual to prepare for the move. Her mother had promised to pick up Kimmie after school and keep her for dinner, safely out from underfoot. And also away from any temptation to smuggle in the cat.

Everything seemed under control, Jan reflected, as she packed last-minute items from the bathroom and kitchen. Yesterday, she'd gathered key personal and financial property to take in her car, and had emptied drawers and cabinets with a sense of déjà vu. She'd performed these same tasks in Houston less than two months ago.

The smelly pile of cushions and ruined furniture had been removed yesterday. Aside from a few new cushions stained beyond salvaging, she didn't miss the lot, except for the dent that replacing them was going to make in her bank account. The scary part was wondering how much she might owe the landlord. Staying at her mom's would save on rent, though, Jan mused.

The movers arrived promptly at six, a trio of young men who operated a discount local service. She'd just finished showing them around and was about to start loading her car when her cell rang.

It was Zack. "Have you moved yet?"

Strange question. "They're carrying the stuff out now."

"Change of plans," he said.

"What do you mean, 'change of plans'?"

He cleared his throat. "Have you talked to Kimmie?"

"About what?" Jan asked. "My mom picked her up after school."

Over the phone, she heard Berry's voice in the background. "When are they coming?"

"Hold on," he said, apparently to Berry. Then, into the phone: "It seems our daughters have arranged for you both to move in here until you can find another place. There was some mention of saving a cat's life."

Faintly, Jan heard Berry's voice again. "Don't forget the bed."

"And a canopy bed that's going to change hands temporarily," Zack noted. "I've hired a sitter for Berry. Okay if I come over?"

"Better hurry," Jan said.

MAKING LAST-MINUTE MAJOR changes in his living arrangements went against the grain for Zack. The bumping and grunting as the movers carted a disassembled bed frame through Jan's empty living room contributed to his sense of losing control.

"I'd suggest we think this over, except that once you move in with your mom, I doubt you'll want to move again in a few days," he explained as they stood out of the way.

She pressed her lips together, clearly trying to process what he'd told her. Kimmie had corralled Berry at lunchtime and persuaded her that moving in together would be a great thing. She'd offered the use of her princess-style bed. This seemed strongly appealing to Berry, as was the prospect of rescuing a stray cat. While Zack wasn't keen on animals, he understood the sympathy factor better, now that he'd seen all those abandoned animals at the shelter.

"Why are you willing to do this?" Jan asked.

Zack had debated with himself before calling her, going so far as to list pros and cons. The pros had won by a slim margin. Despite a sense of unreality, he'd decided to go with his instincts about what was best for the kids.

"It means a lot to both girls, and I'm pleased to see them getting along. Also, this way I can spend more time with Kimmie." Honesty compelled him to add, "Plus I'd rather not go down in family history as a cat murderer."

"Neither would I," Jan retorted grimly. "Now I'm the

bad guy if I say no. And have you taken into account how this will look at work?"

He had. "If tongues are wagging, let them wag as hard as they like."

That startled a smile from her. "What about the logistics of who sleeps where?"

"The girls can share—there's space in Berry's room for two beds. You'll take the guest room. The garage can accommodate any stuff that doesn't fit in the house."

The movers were making short work of Kimmie's furniture, Zack observed. Soon they'd be tackling Jan's. Like it or not, a decision had to be reached quickly.

"I'd like to get closer to Berry, since our lives are entwined now, one way or another," Jan conceded. "But how do you think they'll react when I find another place and we move out? I was hoping to do that soon."

"They'll adjust." Zack hoped so.

"Setting a target date for leaving will reduce the uncertainties," Jan said. "How about early December? That gives me two months to line up a place, and we can be settled by Christmas."

"Fair enough." Speaking of the holidays… "What about Thanksgiving?"

"We spend that at my mother's," Jan replied promptly. "I'm sure you'd both be welcome."

"We eat at my parents' house." A stiff affair, but at least the elder Sargents always invited Rima's brother, for Berry's sake. "We'll work out the details later. Well?"

"I may regret this." Jan twisted a corner of her pink T-shirt. "I don't suppose my mother will mind. I didn't give her a lot of choice about letting us stay there."

Zack remembered Maria Garcia fondly. "I always liked her."

"She liked you, too."

He wished he could count on his own parents to be supportive. Last weekend, when Zack had broken the news about Kimmie's existence, his father had spoken bitterly of Jan's selfishness, with a brief reference to Zack's role in keeping the birth a secret. His mom had simply asked when they could meet their new grandchild, to which he'd responded, "Soon."

Best not to worry about it.

"So that's a yes?" he asked Jan.

Their gazes met for an electric moment. Zack couldn't deny his strong physical attraction, but too many years and too many hurts stood between them. They had to focus on becoming coparents for the girls, and on smoothing the relationship between Berry and Kimmie.

"I'll tell the movers about the new destination," Jan said. "Now we'd better see about catching that cat."

He'd brought Smidge's new carrier. "I came prepared," Zack assured her.

*You must be out of your mind.* Not only did Jan repeat the phrase to herself, she expected to hear it from her mother, as well.

Over the phone, however, Maria merely said, "Kimmie's been telling me about her plans. That girl's quite a go-getter."

"Thanks for being a good sport, Mom."

"All in an excellent cause." Exactly what her mother meant by that, Jan didn't dare ask. "Good luck finding the cat."

In the background, Kimmie called, "Look in the bushes near the clubhouse!"

"I'll do that," Jan responded. The area by the clubhouse, which tenants could rent for parties, should be a good source of discarded or dropped food.

As she clicked off, she saw Zack do the same with his phone. "I called my neighbor, Ilsa Ivy, who runs the animal shelter. She said we could drop the cat at her place and she'll have him neutered."

"That's kind of her." Jan hadn't been looking forward to a night of screeching from the downstairs bathroom, not to mention the potential damage a tomcat could wreak.

While the movers continued working, Jan and Zack went outside into the fading light with the heavy plastic cat carrier and a can of tuna. "There's no guarantee Gorilla will trust me," Jan worried.

"If we don't round him up tonight, the girls will be upset. Besides, I've made all the arrangements," Zack pointed out.

"You're not exactly dressed for cat-catching."

He looked down at his tweed sports coat, polo shirt and pressed slacks. "I'll take my chances."

They rounded a corner and approached the clubhouse, a one-story structure with double glass doors, now firmly shut. Only exterior lights were on. The daytime temperature had hovered near eighty, but nights cooled rapidly in October, making Jan wish she hadn't packed all her sweaters.

"Kimmie isn't supposed to go outside without permission, let alone wander this far," she grumbled.

"I have the impression she doesn't care much for rules." Zack halted, scrutinizing the azalea bushes and calla lilies that edged the building.

"She's a powerhouse when she believes she's right."

"That's not entirely a bad thing," he murmured.

*But you were always so rigid about following rules.* "I thought you believed in walking the straight and narrow."

"She's only seven." Zack crouched and set the carrier

on the concrete. "Does Gorilla have a patch of white on his face?"

"Yes. And on his chest."

He indicated the bushes. "He's watching us."

She heard a whisper of movement and saw a bush quaver. "I completely missed him."

"Those gray-and-white stripes make incredible camouflage."

Having recaptured a few runaway kittens in Houston, Jan had no trouble formulating a strategy. "Let's leave the tuna inside the open carrier. He won't come if we're too close."

"This isn't a trap that will spring by itself," Zack reminded her. "He could run off before we get to him."

"We might beat him to it. If not, he'll enjoy a good meal." Kneeling, Jan popped the flip top. The scent of fish wafted into the air.

The bush twitched again. "He's sticking his nose out." Zack sounded amused.

"He couldn't smell it that fast!" Gorilla must be a dozen feet away.

"A cat's sense of smell is nearly fifteen times as strong as a human's," Zack said, unlatching the metal grill that served as the carrier's gate. "They also have a special scent organ in the roof of their mouths."

Since when had Zack become an expert on cats? "Don't tell me they teach that in medical school."

"Wikipedia." He grinned. "Berry's influence."

Reaching past him, Jan slid the can inside the carrier. As she did so, the shelter of Zack's body enveloped her in a delicious warmth. "There. He'll have to go all the way inside to get a taste of that."

"It'll be hard for him to turn around. Maybe catching him won't be so difficult, after all." Zack touched her shoulder to steady himself in the crouching position.

"Cats can back out fast," Jan warned. "And when they're scared, they sprout claws all over."

"I don't mind the clothes but I wish I'd brought heavy gloves." Zack's forehead furrowed.

"I'll spring the trap." Jan recognized the importance of protecting a surgeon's hands. But the male ego counted for something, too, so she added, "I have more experience at this. We used to provide kitten foster care."

"There is such a thing?"

"You bet."

A short distance away, Jan plopped down on the sidewalk. While it felt hard and cold, she preferred it to the nearby damp strip of grass. "Stay low. We're less threatening that way."

Zack eyed the concrete dubiously, then folded himself down beside her. "You cold?"

"A little."

He slid off his jacket and draped it across her shoulders. His woodsy scent surrounded her. "Better?"

"Much. Thank you."

His long legs stretched beside her shorter ones. The contact felt safe and comforting.

They sat quietly in the twilight. Jan caught a whiff of barbecue from some unseen kitchen, which reminded her she'd eaten only a yogurt for dinner. From a nearby apartment drifted the chatter of a TV news show, and on the walkway, a woman hurried past, high heels clicking.

Gorilla, who'd been creeping closer, beat a hasty retreat into cover. "He's jumpy," Zack murmured.

"That's what comes of living dangerously." She hadn't missed the slash mark on his face, no doubt a souvenir of his latest battle.

"He's footloose and fancy-free." His low voice vibrated in her ear.

"But lonely. Cats have tender hearts." Having grown up around dogs, Jan had taken to felines only at her daughter's insistence and been caught off guard by how affectionate they were.

"And empty stomachs," he said, peering at their quarry.

Gorilla had once again crept from his leafy refuge. He inched toward the carrier, every muscle taut as if he were stalking prey.

Zack slid an arm around Jan. "You were swaying," he said softy. "I'm afraid you'll lose your balance."

What a ridiculous remark. "I'm sitting down."

"Shhh. You'll scare the cat."

Jan gave him a light poke in the ribs as payback for his teasing. In response, he tightened his grip, and rather than struggle, she leaned against him. After all, he must be chilly without his coat, and it felt good to rest her head on his shoulder.

The cat braced, studying them. "It's okay," Jan told it. "You can trust us."

"We come in peace," Zack added.

The cat tensed.

"Shhh." It was her turn to issue a warning.

"Sorry." He nuzzled her hair.

Gorilla took their measure, the temptation to flee obviously counterbalanced by the lure of the tuna. His eyes glowed with reflected light.

As they awaited his next move, Zack's lips traced Jan's temple, sending a pleasurable tingling through her body. She'd missed this sense of intimacy, this instinctive reaction. None of the other men she'd dated over the years had inspired a response that even came close. Perhaps that was why none of the relationships had lasted past a few outings.

She rubbed her cheek against the stubble that sprouted along his jaw. When Zack's finger touched her chin, she lifted her face obligingly and parted her lips in welcome.

A flick of his tongue sparked an electric current. Her arms encircling him, Jan relished the strength of his body and the pounding of his heart, a match for her own speeding pulse. As his mouth probed hers, flames flickered across her skin, and her breasts tightened as if he were cupping them in his hands.

She wanted more, but the awareness that they were in public view, although obscured by shadows, halted her. What if the movers came by? And what about their mission?

As she drew back, she felt Zack's grip tighten. Then, with a reluctant sigh, he eased off. Had it been a mistake? It didn't feel like one to Jan. Yet with so much hanging in the balance, she knew they'd be wise to let it go.

A few feet away, Gorilla was eating the tuna, body bunched inside the carrier with his tail flicking outside. He'd taken advantage of their distraction.

*Gotcha!* Rising to a crouch, Jan crossed the short distance, pushed the tail inside and snapped the door shut.

A protesting meow filled the air. The cage rocked as the cat tried to back out, then twisted awkwardly.

"Sorry," Jan told Gorilla, who regarded her as if she'd betrayed his trust. She felt guilty for tricking him. "You'll be better off now, honest."

His protesting yowl shattered the evening peace. "That's one ticked-off cat," Zack observed as he got to his feet. "Good job, Jan."

"I feel like a dirty rat," she admitted.

"But you're on the side of the angels." He picked up

the carrier and they headed toward the parking area. The cat thrashed about and then froze, obviously terrified by its unstable environment.

"Dare I hope you brought a blanket to protect your van?" Jan asked.

"I keep one in the back. For picnics and beach trips with Berry."

Under a security light Jan used her phone to snap a shot of Gorilla's face peering between the bars. "To prove we really did catch him, since he'll be gone for a few days."

"Kimmie won't take your word for it?"

"Yes, but she'll worry. Ask me ten times if I'm sure I got the right cat, that kind of thing." Jan knew her daughter well. "She has maternal instincts."

"I guess Berry might, too." He took a picture with his phone. "In case your shot doesn't do the trick."

With Gorilla safely stowed in his van, Zack helped Jan tote her computer and suitcases to her car. He tucked a few large items into his vehicle, as well. She would stay to lock up and guide the movers to his house while Zack dropped off Gorilla.

The carrier was wrapped in a blanket with room for air, and the cat had calmed down by the time Zack slid behind the wheel. It mewed plaintively as Jan took a final peek.

"You'll be happy in your new home," she told it. "I promise."

She hoped the same would be true for all four humans, who'd just taken a leap of faith. It was only temporary, Jan reminded herself, and strode back to her apartment.

## Chapter Twelve

The administrator's secretary posted the weekly rankings for the Hope Challenge in the doctors' lounge at noon on Fridays. With about six weeks left, Zack had been edging upward, reaching third position behind Owen Tartikoff and Mark Rayburn.

Teeth gritted, he stared at the latest list, which dropped him to number four. How unfair, especially now that he was adding patients and his tally of successful conceptions had been improving. Previously, Zack had devoted a lot of time to learning the newest microsurgical techniques involved in egg harvesting, transfer and implantation, working with Dr. T, who got credit for those patients' successes.

He'd expected to vie for the second spot this week or next. Instead, he found a new name above his.

Dr. Cole Rattigan.

The urologist had arrived a few months ago to head the male-fertility program and was doing an impressive job. But since when did men get pregnant?

Scowling, Zack glanced away and met the sympathetic gaze of Dr. Nora Franco, the only other person in the lounge. Working part-time since returning from maternity leave, the blonde obstetrician fell near the bottom of the rankings. However, she shared a practice with Paige, who was in fifth position, and both supported the proposed grant program.

"Guess you're not thrilled at being edged by a newbie," she remarked.

"How does that work, anyway?" Zack asked. "He treats men."

"You must have missed the email. Couples count twice if Cole treats the husband, so two doctors get credit." Nora shrugged. "My guess is Dr. T tossed him into the mix to shake things up."

The fertility head's glee in throwing curve balls at the staff was well-known. "Any idea where Cole would donate the prize?"

"I've barely met the guy." Nora transferred her attention to the posted list of on-call assignments. Although one staff obstetrician worked a regular night shift, the others took turns on weekends. Recently, Nora had agreed to join the roster even though she was only a part-timer.

"I didn't realize…" She hesitated.

"Something wrong?"

Deep breath. "I've been proud of how well I've been balancing medicine and motherhood, but… Zack, I hate to ask a favor, especially while you're adjusting to a new family situation." Nora waved her hand apologetically. "I didn't mean to bring that up."

"I'm used to it." In the past four days, as word of his living arrangement spread, Zack had grown accustomed to speculative glances and to the conversational lull that greeted his arrival in the cafeteria. "How can I help you?"

"Neo is having tubes put in his ears this afternoon, and I'm scheduled to be on call tomorrow night." Neo was Nora's eleven-month-old son. "Leo's handling a tough case and might have to go on stakeout." Her husband, the brother of hospital attorney Tony Franco, worked as a police detective.

Normally, Zack would have readily offered to replace her. But was that fair to his family?

After a few days on their best behavior, the girls had begun picking fights with each other since yesterday's arrival of a much mellower Gorilla. Kimmie carted the neutered cat around the house, declaring she didn't want anyone else to touch him. Meanwhile Berry had become intensely protective of Smidge and accused the larger cat of intimidating her baby.

"My sister-in-law and I usually sit for each other, but Brady has a cold and I don't think Neo should be around him so soon after surgery. And Paige is on her honeymoon." Nora regarded Zack wistfully.

What kind of person was he turning into, for heaven's sake? Nora shouldn't have to leave her son with a sitter the day after his operation. "Of course I'll do it."

Relief flashed across her face. "Are you sure?"

"No problem." On the posted chart, Zack substituted his name and initialed the change. "I'll tell the delivery-room staff."

"I can take care of that." Nora hugged him. "You're a sweetheart. And I'll cover for you whenever you like."

"No hurry." Zack had always taken on-call responsibilities in stride, and so had Berry. Of course, until recently she'd enjoyed spending the night with little Rachel.

He was about to call Mary Beth Ellroy to see if she could take his daughter on Saturday, when it struck him that Jan could watch both girls. While they'd left the girls' regular after-school arrangements in place, this was different. Sleeping in her own bed meant less disruption for Berry. So why did the prospect trouble him?

Jan wasn't Berry's stepmother, or anything beyond a

temporary housemate. How would Berry react to being left in her care overnight? And, if they grew attached, to her departure in a few months?

Being banished to Mary Beth's house might be even worse, however. Checking his watch, Zack calculated he could spare a few minutes to discuss this with Jan.

Downstairs, he was glad to see no trace of the nosy receptionist, who must be at lunch. As Zack approached Jan's office, however, the adjacent door opened and he found himself face-to-face with Cole Rattigan.

Zack gave the other man a polite nod. Although only a few years older than Zack and about the same height, the urologist carried his stockier frame with a self-satisfied air. Understandable, since Rattigan had been wooed by Dr. T due to his impressive résumé and national reputation, but his air of superiority did nothing to make him more likable.

"Did you want to talk to me?" the other man asked. "I was on my way out."

Might as well seize the moment. "Congratulations. You're in third place."

Cole blinked, apparently baffled. "In what exactly?"

"The Hope Challenge," Zack clarified.

Understanding dawned. "Oh, that. What about it?"

The urologist wasn't making this easy. Still, Zack could hardly expect him to care as much about the outcome as those who had a more vested interest. "You've heard about our competing propositions for the prize money?"

"Someone mentioned it," Cole said vaguely. "The winner's free to donate it wherever he or she wishes, I gather."

Was he deliberately being provocative? Hard to tell. "A grant program could mean a lot to our patients. Men as well as women," Zack noted.

"Dr. T's the one you have to persuade. He's practically a shoo-in. Or Rayburn, but since his wife's behind the counseling center, I expect you're out of luck there," the man said, as casually as if they were handicapping a football game. "Catch you later, Jack."

With a clap on the shoulder, off he went. Zack didn't bother to correct his mistake about the name.

Jan peeked out her door, eyes dancing. "Is there steam coming out of your ears?"

"You heard that?" Of course she had. "Damn."

"For what it's worth, I'd choose the grant program, but my opinion doesn't count. What can I do for you?"

Zack glanced around, a habit that had become second nature. Since they'd spread the news of their shared parenthood and living arrangements, they'd been extra careful to avoid any personal discussions.

Jan indicated the empty desk and the open doors around the perimeter. "Everyone's out," she said. "Come in and tell me what's up."

Keeping an eye out for Caroline's return, Zack explained about Nora's request. "I suppose I should have checked with you first. You might have other plans."

"Frankly, I'm delighted."

He hadn't anticipated that reaction. "You're delighted I'll be away?"

"Touchy, touchy." She chuckled. "It's just that, so far, I haven't had any time alone with the girls."

"And that's a problem?"

"I'm not criticizing you," she said. "Why so tense?"

"It's the damn contest." *Well, not entirely.* "And I'm concerned about Berry. You can see how things are unraveling."

"You mean because the girls are sniping at each other?"

Jan leaned against the edge of her desk. "It's a relief. I've been wondering when the gloves would come off."

How could she take this so lightly? If people didn't control their emotions, the result could be open antagonism and even estrangement. "They need both of us there to…" He nearly said "lay down the law," which was what his father would have said. Disturbed by that observation, he amended it to "Mediate. And reassure them."

"This is their period of adjustment," Jan advised. "They have to work it out."

"They aren't married." The psychology classes Zack had taken to help counsel patients had explained about the phases marriages went through.

"Any serious relationship goes through a bumpy period as people figure out where they stand," Jan countered.

"Not necessarily." His and Rima's first-year adjustment had gone smoothly. Of course, Zack had made allowances for any differences due to her ill health, and she'd been a gentle soul like her daughter.

"Most of the time," Jan persisted. "People instinctively push the boundaries. It's part of figuring out how far the other person can be trusted. Besides, the girls could use some time away from you."

"I don't see that at all." Kimmie had already spent seven years away from him. That was more than enough.

She raised her hands in a pacifying gesture. "When you're present, they feel like rivals for your love. This might give them a chance to find common ground. I'm more of a neutral party."

Zack wasn't convinced. "You're hardly neutral. You and Kimmie have a lifelong bond that leaves Berry on the outside." His little girl ought to feel she had at least one parent in her corner, especially in her own home.

"She and I are part of each other's lives now," Jan said.

"I expect we always will be, because of your involvement with Kimmie. Berry's aware we're moving out in December. If we establish a relationship now, I can continue to be her friend. That's all I'm suggesting."

The girls had absorbed that timetable with no obvious concern. Zack wasn't sure they grasped what it was going to mean. Still, he *would* like his daughters to view each other as sisters, and that meant giving Jan a continuing role with Berry. "I guess she can cope with having you babysit. Beyond that, we'll have to see."

Her hands formed fists, but with a clear effort of will Jan flexed them and settled back against the desk. "I'll be fair to both girls," she said quietly.

"We can play this by ear," Zack conceded. "I appreciate your willingness to supervise her."

"Glad to."

"My on-call shift starts at eight o'clock, so I'll be home for dinner. Any idea what we're having?"

"Spaghetti?" It was one of Jan's fallbacks.

"They'll like that." But he wasn't crazy about serving all those carbs. They ought to work out a system for meal planning. "Over the weekend I'll draw up a list of healthy meals. Turkey burgers, chicken sausage, some vegetarian dishes. You can add to it, of course, and we'll take turns shopping and cooking. How's that sound?"

"Fine." She nodded toward the outer office, where Caroline had put in an appearance. "Thanks for your input, Dr. Sargent."

"My pleasure."

He was halfway down the hall before he registered that they'd quarreled and patched it up. Maybe they were having their own period of adjustment. If so, they'd just weathered a storm.

That felt good.

TOO RESTLESS TO STAY in her office, Jan spent the rest of Friday reviewing the hospital facilities available to the egg-donor bank. Because they were scattered all over the building, she had to work on visualizing the project as a cohesive entity.

Originally, Dr. Rayburn had explained, the corporation that owned the medical center had intended to purchase a nearby dental office building to remodel for the fertility program. When those plans fell through, unused space in the hospital had been reconfigured and upgraded.

Thus, her office and Melissa's were on the main floor, while Dr. T's and Alec Denny's occupied a suite on the fifth. On the second floor, two operating rooms were set aside for fertility surgeries, along with rooms for egg retrieval and sperm donation. In the basement, major remodeling had upgraded air-and-water-filtration systems to accommodate the embryology and other laboratories that Alec oversaw.

Today's tour sparked new insights and ideas, even though she'd viewed everything before. And pounding the staircase instead of taking the elevator wore the edge off her agitation. She was pleased she'd held on to her temper with Zack, and she sympathized with his fears for Berry. If only he were more willing to trust.

Not that she didn't have some issues in that department, as well. For years she'd raised their child alone, ignoring occasional yearnings to have a man protect and help her. A man to laugh and cuddle with like on the night they captured Gorilla.

Jan hadn't met anyone who came close to fitting that description, except for Zack. Despite the undeniable physical response he could still awaken in her, the divide between them loomed as large as ever.

*Never mind that.* The immediate challenge was to reconcile the girls and the cats. And to demonstrate that being around Jan was good for Berry. Besides, tomorrow should go smoothly. With Zack leaving close to the girls' bedtime, what could go wrong?

On Saturday morning, Berry played at a friend's house and Kimmie enjoyed a chance to play with Smidge. With permission, she took the kitten onto the patio, since it was too small to run off. Indoors, Gorilla jumped into Jan's lap and curled there while she worked on her laptop with a view of her daughter through the sliding glass door.

Zack joined Kimmie for a while, then took Berry to a park where, he'd explained, they liked to run laps on a track. When they got home, Berry seemed calm and happy...until she learned Kimmie had taken the kitten outside.

"He's *mine.*" Berry's jaw jutted forward as she stood in the middle of the den.

Jan shot Kimmie a warning glance. Her daughter, clearly on the verge of arguing, shrugged instead. "Whatever."

"Don't you do it again!"

"Nap time," Jan announced to head off a squabble. "Who wants to sleep in my room?"

"Me!" Kimmie shouted.

Berry folded her arms. "I'd rather play with Smidge in *my* room."

"It's my room, too. Don't forget you're sleeping in *my* bed," Kimmie added.

"It's Berry's bed as long as we stay here," Jan corrected.

"I never liked it anyway," her daughter shot back.

From the kitchen table where he was reading on his tablet computer, Zack glanced up. "Naps sound like a good idea."

"I'm too old to nap," Berry retorted.

Talking back to her father? That was a new development, Jan gathered, and from Zack's expression, obviously not a welcome one. "Then you can have quiet time instead," she responded. "There's a new fashion magazine on the table over there, if that's all right with your father."

Zack raised no objection. "Okay!" Berry snatched up the magazine and ran off.

Kimmie lingered. "Read to me." She peered at her mother appealingly.

Too appealingly. Much as Jan enjoyed reading to her daughter, she didn't want to show what might appear to be favoritism.

"This is my quiet time, too," Jan responded. "Besides, the more you read on your own, the better you'll get at it."

"Whatever." That seemed to be Kimmie's new favorite word. It was rapidly becoming Jan's *un*favorite.

Zack watched his younger daughter depart. "You managed that well."

"Thanks." Jan opened the dishwasher, which they'd run after lunch, and began putting away the clean dishes. "Period of adjustment. If I repeat that phrase often enough, it should keep me from screaming."

"Let's all do something together when they finish quiet time." His phone rang. "Did I tempt fate by saying that?"

"Possibly."

As it turned out, several of his patients had gone into labor and were requesting his personal attention, he explained after ending the conversation. Although it was three o'clock and he wasn't due in for five hours, obstetricians had to be flexible. Also, the doctor on duty had his hands full.

"Some days are like that." Zack switched off his tablet. "I'm grateful I don't have to rely on Mrs. Ellroy to watch Berry this afternoon. Jan, I appreciate your help."

"My pleasure." She hoped that would be the case.

"Good thing I keep a bag packed." He'd explained he slept in the doctors' on-call room on nights like this. "I'll go tell the girls goodbye."

"See you in the morning." The prospect of spending the night here without him bothered Jan a little. Funny how in less than a week she'd grown accustomed to being around Zack in the evenings after the girls went to bed. Mostly, they read in companionable silence in the den, catching up on professional journals, or watched documentaries and news shows.

Occasionally they discussed a matter of public policy, disagreeing on details but agreeing in principle. Even when they weren't talking, the room came alive with his breathing, his movements, his thoughts.

During the night, when she awoke, she felt his presence across the second-floor hallway. Even asleep, he made her feel safer.

It was only one night. She'd be fine.

Still, when she heard Zack's car pull out of the garage, Jan felt a sudden emptiness in the house. Not only because she missed him, but because of what she faced during the hours to come.

She'd been confident she could keep the peace and transform the girls into lifelong friends—not to mention becoming a sort of aunt to Berry. Now she was about to be put to the test.

That ought to keep her too busy to get lonely.

Taking advantage of the break, Jan finished emptying the dishwasher. She was getting accustomed to the arrangement of the cabinets and drawers. Since Zack was well supplied with cooking gear she'd left her own stuff in boxes.

Turning to her laptop she checked rental listings in Safe Harbor and marked a few that allowed pets. However, until she received the repair bill from the landlord, she hesitated to make a financial commitment. Zack had declined her offer to pay him rent, for which she was grateful. But if she owed thousands of dollars…

Upstairs the floor creaked beneath footsteps. "Dibs on the bathroom!" came Berry's voice.

"I gotta go!"

"Me, too, and I was here first!" From the sound of it, they were scuffling.

For heaven's sakes. This house contained three bathrooms, but the girls chose to fight over the one between the bedrooms.

Gathering her resolve, Jan closed the laptop and went to intervene.

# Chapter Thirteen

By the scheduled start of his on-call shift Zack had delivered four babies. Each birth filled him with joy and a sense of privilege at witnessing a miracle.

How ironic that he'd missed the birth of his own daughter. Both his daughters, although he could hardly have attended Berry's. In the long run, the circumstances of their births weren't what mattered, Zack reflected. He was lucky to have them in his life, and to be a part of his patients' special experiences.

On the downside, it was eight-fifteen and he had not yet eaten dinner. He was about to descend from the third floor to the cafeteria when one of the labor nurses came chasing after him.

"Mrs. Murdock's baby is crowning!" she cried. "We need you fast. Dr. Rayburn's coming but she can't hold out for ten minutes."

"Thanks." Swinging back, Zack followed her at a run.

Sarah Ann Murdock was a thirty-two-year-old patient of Dr. Rayburn's. She'd been admitted three hours earlier in labor with her first baby. The administrator, who lived close to the hospital, had left instructions he planned to deliver the baby himself and had been notified to stand by.

The last time Zack checked, he'd estimated the patient

had several more hours of labor. Obviously, she'd progressed more quickly than expected.

There was no sign of any problem with mother or baby, the nurse assured him. "She claims women in her family deliver fast, even the first time. We should have listened."

"Guess so."

He scrubbed and hurried into the delivery room, where the nurses were urging the distraught mother to restrain her urge to push. Hovering near his wife, the husband spotted Zack with obvious relief. "Honey! The doctor's here."

Sarah Ann Murdock glared at Zack. "You aren't Dr. Rayburn!"

"He's on his way. We didn't realize you were going to set an Olympic speed record." Zack confirmed everything seemed normal and on track with mother and baby. "You can push now."

"Thank goodness!"

A few minutes later, she was cradling her healthy blanket-wrapped son while Dad snapped pictures. Mark Rayburn hurried in, dark eyes apologetic as he addressed the patient. "I hear you decided I was too much of a slowpoke. How do you feel, Sarah Ann?"

"Like I just gave birth to a whale." Tears of happiness ran down her face. "But it was worth it."

The couple had tried for years to have children—Zack had seen her records. After surgery on blocked fallopian tubes failed to do the trick, they'd succeeded at last thanks to in vitro fertilization.

"Next time I'll come the instant you go into labor," Mark assured her. "And never mind what else I'm doing." He'd once explained to Zack that he would quit the post of administrator if it required giving up patient care.

Husband and wife exchanged glances. "There won't

be a next time," the husband said regretfully. "We'll be paying the bills for this one until he's ready for college."

"We plan to relish every minute," his wife added.

"Got a name picked out?" Zack asked.

"Simon," both parents said.

"Good name." Mark smiled.

As Zack departed, a nurse brought him a turkey sandwich. "We've got two more in labor and another was just admitted," she told him.

"This was thoughtful. What do I owe you?"

"I'll put it on your tab." No doubt he'd run up more food bills before the night was over, he reflected as he thanked her.

Zack was eating the sandwich in the doctors' lounge when the administrator found him. "Just wanted to say you did a great job in there."

"Beautiful kid."

Mark regarded the bulletin board with the contest rankings. "You and I ought to share this one."

"It was your pregnancy," Zack said. "Deliveries don't count."

The older man's black eyebrows drew together. "I hate to see couples give up on completing their families because of money."

The patient's situation must have touched a nerve. "Are you referring to the grant program?"

"It's a good idea. Wish we had one in place."

"Puts you in a tough spot," Zack observed.

"Samantha and I don't necessarily think alike." That was as close as the administrator came to admitting he disagreed about allocating the prize money to the counseling center. "Frankly, I'm thinking of taking myself out of the running. It's a conflict of interest."

Much as Zack would like to move up in the standings,

he disagreed. "It's not as if you're a judge. Either your patients get pregnant or they don't, and where to donate the money is the winner's choice."

"I should think you'd encourage me to step back."

"It's Dr. T who's likely to win." Zack broke off. "Never mind. He has the same right as anyone else."

"That could be debated." Mark frowned at the chart. "The point of the contest is to build staff morale and generate some positive publicity."

"No matter who wins, the corporation's money will go to a good cause," Zack acknowledged. "We could look for other sources to fund a grant program."

"I'll give that some thought. But a major donation would certainly get it off to a strong start."

"Guess I'll just have to inspire my patients to greater fertility." Zack gave the administrator a wry grin.

"You may develop a sense of humor yet."

*I thought I had one already.* Was he really perceived as being that stern?

With a wave Mark was off, no doubt to spell his wife on overnight duty with the triplets. Meanwhile, Zack recalled, Jan was dealing with their two kids.

Not theirs, except temporarily. All the same, he appreciated her effort. And hoped she was in touch with her sense of humor, because she was likely to need it.

How many ways could two little girls find to pester each other and make life miserable for the adult in charge? By early evening Jan had lost count.

They squabbled about who got to play with the kitten and how much time Gorilla could spend in the den, which required banishing Smidge to the bedroom. They argued over what to have for dinner, forcing Jan to make an executive decision. The girls made short work of the home-made veggie pizza and salad with low-fat ranch dressing, but as if unable to bear more than a few moments of peace, they fought over the last half scoop of sherbet. Jan ate it herself, then felt childish for doing so.

She tried to reason with them, together and separately. Both listened sullenly, then went and picked another quarrel.

While she disliked using TV as a babysitter, Jan made a last-ditch attempt to settle them in front of a documentary about parrots, one of Kimmie's favorite films. Her daughter promptly sprawled next to Jan on the couch and refused to make space for Berry.

"You're my mom," she declared. "I get to sit here!"

"There's room for both of you on either side."

"Oh, she can sit there. Who cares? She's just a baby." Arms folded, Berry sank into an armchair and plopped her feet on the coffee table.

If the girls shot each other any more laser-sharp glares, Jan was likely to get burns. "That does it." She turned off the DVD. "We're going for a walk."

"It's cold out!" Kimmie protested.

"Dad and I already exercised today," Berry grumbled.

They both aimed their objections at Jan, which she considered a step in the right direction. Having them unite against her represented progress of a sort. An uncomfortable sort.

"You're fighting like a pair of tomcats," she told them. "Let's see who claims to own the sidewalk."

"It was my neighborhood first!" Berry said.

Jan laughed.

"What?" the girl demanded.

"Yeah, what's so funny? I mean, besides her face," Kimmie added.

"Get your jackets on, now!" The exercise ought to take the edge off their restlessness, and Zack would approve.

Jan admired his insistence on healthy habits for Berry, even if he was a little rigid. Faced with time pressures, she too often took the easy way out with Kimmie, eating fast food and collapsing in front of the TV.

Zack was a good influence. Now if she could keep the girls from becoming enemies… Until today, she'd believed the two would enjoy being sisters, but she was having doubts. What if their antagonism hardened into a long-lasting rift, as Zack feared?

*You can do this. Don't give up.*

Outside, the cool air raised another protest from Kimmie, which inspired Berry to call her a wimp. "No talking," Jan said. "First girl to spot a stray cat gets a sugar-free candy." She'd brought a pocketful.

The girls fell silent, peering into the twilight. Older homes, many in the California bungalow style with old-fashioned porches, featured clumps of birds of paradise and calla lilies. Here and there between cottages rose newer Mediterranean-style structures, fences draped with bougainvillea, and Cape Cod houses like Zack's, planted with roses. Lots of places for kitties to prowl.

As the girls kept a lookout, Jan noted some residents had raised Halloween banners on their flagpoles. This must be a fun area to go trick-or-treating, although she usually took Kimmie to a party at a church or community center, to be safe. She was wondering about Zack's plans when she recalled he didn't let Berry eat most types of candy.

Jan supposed she might restrict Kimmie's sugar intake this year, but it didn't seem right to ban candy entirely. Another battle loomed between the girls. And possibly between Jan and Zack.

"There's one!" Berry cried.

"I saw it first!"

The girls pointed to a tortoiseshell cat skulking around a street corner. "You both win." Jan handed each a wrapped candy. "No littering. Put the trash in your pocket or give it to me."

"Can we play this some more?" Kimmie asked.

"You bet."

They had just rounded the corner when Kimmie said, "Oh, look!"

Toward them strolled a tall woman with thick gray hair. Alongside her, on leashes, paced a wiry terrier bouncing with energy and an easy-gaited, flop-eared pooch triple its size.

"Those are dogs, not cats," Berry sneered.

"I know that," Kimmie returned. "That's Ilsa Ivy. She runs the animal shelter."

*A good person to meet.* "Hi," Jan said as the woman approached. "I'm new to the neighborhood." They introduced themselves and shook hands, while the dogs waited obediently.

"You remember me!" Kimmie said confidently.

"I do, indeed."

"And this is Berry, Zack Sargent's older daughter." Seeing Ilsa's confused expression, Jan decided to explain. "My daughter, Kimmie, and I are staying with the Sargents until we find a place that accepts pets. We own Gorilla, the cat you got neutered. Thank you for taking care of him."

"Always glad to help an animal."

"Can we pet the dogs?" Kimmie asked.

"Yes, and thank you for asking."

Kimmie knelt to pat the smaller animal, which wagged its tail so hard it nearly flew into orbit. It also let out a few high-pitched barks as if to justify its name, which Ilsa said was Yappy. Berry gravitated to the calmer Pal, a Labrador-shepherd mix that tolerated her hug indulgently.

"They're very well behaved." Jan could tell these canines had lovable personalities.

"Both former strays," Ilsa announced. "You can't believe how much work it took before they got along."

"Like me and Berry," Kimmie said from her kneeling position on the sidewalk.

"I have to share my bedroom," Berry complained.

"That can't be easy," the shelter operator sympathized. "You know, I have a project you could both work on, if your parents agree. It might give you girls something in common and it would help the animals."

"Okay!" Kimmie didn't hesitate.

Berry proved more cautious. "What is it?"

"Instead of asking for candy on Halloween, some children raise funds for good causes," Ilsa told them. "Our shelter may have to close if we can't fix our plumbing and air-conditioning systems."

"They need about a million dollars," Kimmie said.

"Twenty thousand, but it feels like a million. And that doesn't include expanding the kennels and our spay-neuter program." The older woman paused to pat each dog and praise it for sitting quietly. "We've made up fliers to distribute, requesting donations instead of candy and explaining what it's for. Even if people can't donate now, they might help later."

Jan had to admit the idea offered a welcome solution to the candy dilemma. And judging by how intently both girls listened, they might be willing to work together. "What do you kids think?"

"No candy?" Despite her disappointed tone, Kimmie squared her little shoulders. "Okay."

"Can we still wear costumes?" Berry asked.

"That's up to your parents." Ilsa regarded Jan questioningly.

"Costumes, yes. As for the fund-raising, I'll have to clear it with Zack." Judging by the way the girls were jumping up and down, she doubted he'd have much choice.

"I get to be a kitty!" Kimmie announced.

"I'm older! I get to pick first!" Berry shot back.

"You can both be cats," Jan said.

"But you must cooperate." Ilsa gave Jan a conspiratorial smile. "If you fight that sets a bad example for the dogs. See how well they're getting along?"

"Yeah." Kimmie gave Yappy another pat. "We can both be cats."

"I want orange stripes like Smidge," Berry announced.

"And I'll be gray with white patches."

"We'd better finish our walk and start planning our costumes." Much as she'd like to wait for Zack's okay, Jan decided to capitalize on the girls' willingness to work together.

"You can download the flier from our website and run off your own copies," Ilsa said. "That would save us money."

"Of course." Jan was grateful for Ilsa's suggestion. "I'm not sure how much we'll collect, but…"

"Everything helps." With a friendly nod, the woman clucked to the dogs. They jumped up and strolled away at her heels.

Jan kept that image in mind. While she didn't expect one project to transform Kimmie and Berry into best pals, it was a start.

## Chapter Fourteen

Usually, Zack fell instantly into a deep sleep between deliveries. The noise from the hospital hallway, the uncomfortable stiffness of the bunk beds in the on-call room—none of that mattered.

This night, though, he lay awake worrying about Berry. Had he yielded to his own convenience without adequately weighing what it meant to let her stay home with Jan? Sure, sleeping in her own bed might increase her sense of security, but what about the security of familiar arrangements with Mrs. Ellroy? If Jan failed to reconcile the girls, Berry might feel isolated and embattled in her own home.

Maybe Zack shouldn't have let Jan and Kimmie move in so quickly. Or, more likely, he ought to quiet his brain and get some sleep.

Exhaustion finally won out.

After the shift ended at eight o'clock in the morning, he drove home under a cloud of apprehension. As father to both girls he loved them equally, but Berry seemed the more vulnerable of the pair.

From the garage, Zack used the connecting door to the kitchen. He half expected to find the kids eating breakfast but the room was empty.

Hearing the murmur of voices from the den he moved forward quietly. A flash of sunshine through the sliding glass door dimmed his sight, and he shifted to one side. When his vision cleared, he saw the girls and Jan sitting on the floor, half-hidden by the armchairs and couch. They were studying her laptop, open on the coffee table.

Kimmie wore a pair of jeans and a T-shirt he recognized as belonging to Berry. She in turn had thrown on a flower-printed pink top he'd never seen before.

"That's dorky." Kimmie pointed to the screen. "Who ever heard of a pink kitty?"

"And cats don't wear dresses with pictures of kittens on them," Berry added derisively. "What a dumb costume."

Were they arguing? Zack tensed, surprised they hadn't noticed his presence but willing to eavesdrop until he got a better sense of what was going on.

"Just wanted to be sure you guys hadn't changed your minds since last night." Jan closed the computer. "Okay, so, Berry, you don't mind if Kimmie wears your black leotard and tights?"

"They're too small anyway," came the response. "I get new ones, right? The same color as Smidge?"

"I can't guarantee we'll find that exact color, but we'll try," Jan answered.

They might not have noticed the new arrival, but someone had. Across the carpet stalked a furry gray cat, tail twitching. Gorilla stared up at Zack, who felt as if he was being assessed as a potential male rival.

Seriously? He had to face down a cat?

Apparently his stare did the trick. Gorilla sat at Zack's feet, bobbed his head and distinctly said, "Meow." Not "mrrr" or some random meowlike noise, but articulate syllables. "Me-ow."

*I obviously didn't get enough sleep last night.*

"He wants to be picked up," Kimmie called.

"Daddy!" Despite her enthusiastic cry, Berry remained seated. "We're going to be cats for Halloween."

"And collect money for the shelter," Kimmie added.

"We're going to buy cat masks and paint them like Smidge and Gorilla." Berry's words tumbled out eagerly.

"And make tails!" Kimmie said.

"Hope you don't mind," Jan put in.

"Mind? This is amazing." The girls weren't merely co-existing, they were enthusiastically joining forces.

Words flew at him from his daughters. Took a walk… ran into Mrs. Ivy…save the animals…money not candy…

They glowed with high spirits. As for Jan, her cheeks were a lively shade of pink, and she looked radiant. *A natural mom,* Zack thought. This was the kind of maternal influence Berry needed and had been missing.

"You guys had quite an evening. Show me what you're planning, and then we have to get ready for church."

"Can we come, too?" Kimmie asked.

"If it's okay with your mom."

"That would be great," Jan said.

"You'll know some of the congregation from the hospital," Zack noted, before turning his attention to his daughters. "You girls planning to wear each other's clothes to the service?"

They scrambled to their feet. "We'll go change!" He wasn't sure which of them said that. Maybe both.

As they raced out, Jan got up and brushed off the jeans that clung to her rounded curves. "Before I get dressed…"

"Thank you." Zack caught her hands in his. "Frankly, I was worried."

"I meant to consult about all these decisions…"

"You made good choices." Just being near her filled him with the same glow he'd seen on his daughters' faces.

"I just…" The purpose burning in her gaze warned

Zack the day's revelations weren't over. "We've made a start. Now I think we should spend Thanksgiving together as a family. Here in this house."

"My family has its traditions. Not that they can't be changed," he added. Events at his parents' home tended to be more funereal than festive.

"We should keep the girls together. And if we celebrate here, we can include both sets of relatives." Jan studied him hopefully. "The girls can help decorate and set up. It will mean a lot to them."

Zack liked the idea. Still, his parents hadn't even met Kimmie yet, an issue he intended to remedy soon. "You aren't concerned about how my folks might act? My dad can be difficult."

"He never liked me," Jan conceded. "But he never really got to know me." The couple had been working such long hours, they hadn't even had an engagement party or begun making wedding plans before their breakup.

"They took a while to warm up to Rima, too." Zack's wife had expended a lot of effort to connect with them. Having lost her own parents, she'd considered them important for Berry. His mother had responded in her usual low-key manner, and eventually his father had unbent enough to greet Rima with a hug each time they met.

"Surely they'll want to spend Thanksgiving with both their granddaughters," Jan pointed out.

"What about your mom? She'd probably want us all at her place." An invitation to dinner at the Garcias' used to mean a table crowded with home-cooked dishes, surrounded by family photos and mementos on the walls and sideboard.

"Arthritis slows her down these days. I bet she'll be grateful not to shoulder so much of the work. And I'll enlist my brother's support. Seriously, everyone needs to get acquainted."

"Including Berry's uncle?" Maintaining family ties with Edgar mattered to Zack. "My parents always invite him."

"Of course!"

Her hands still rested between his. Standing this close tempted him to bend down and brush his mouth across hers.

*The girls will be back any minute.* "You won't be living here next year. What kind of expectations..."

"Let next year take care of itself." Her dark eyes glimmered with a trace of tears. "It's only been two Thanksgivings since we lost my dad. You never know what's going to happen. Let's enjoy who and where we are right now."

Despite his longing to carve out a tradition that would last until the girls grew up, Zack accepted the idea. "I'll persuade my side if you'll handle yours."

"Done." Her smile outshone the sunlight pouring into the room. Then she was gone, leaving a warmth in his hands that faded too quickly.

Turkey. Stuffing. Zack pictured a long table crowded with tasty dishes and lined with beloved faces. One thing was certain: he would take lots of pictures. As Jan said, you never knew what the future might bring.

BY THE WEEK OF THANKSGIVING Jan felt as if she'd been running at full speed for a month. But such wonderful things had happened that she didn't mind.

At the hospital, her friend Erica delivered a beautiful eight-pound-three-ounce baby boy named Jordan. Meanwhile, the Hope Challenge was nearing its conclusion with doctors Tartikoff and Rayburn in the lead, and Zack and

Cole Rattigan vying for third. Amid the mounting anticipation, gossip about Jan and Zack had fallen off the radar.

At home they cooperated smoothly. Buoyed by plans for the holiday, she and Zack took turns cooking and coordinated the girls' activities. With his permission and credit card, Jan had taken Berry shopping for darling new clothes, while Kimmie tried harder to follow rules because she liked pleasing her father. Even the cats resolved their territorial disputes and often slept curled together.

After some initial reluctance, grandparents on both sides agreed to have dinner at Zack's house, with everyone bringing their favorite dishes. And although Jan hadn't had a chance to meet with the Sargents, Zack reported his parents had welcomed Kimmie with open arms.

If anything, they'd gone overboard. When he took her for a visit they showered their new granddaughter with gifts, including a doll and a teddy bear. It apparently didn't occur to them to buy anything for Berry, who'd stayed home. On their return, Kimmie had given her the doll, so her feelings were spared.

"I hope they don't spoil Thanksgiving by doting on their genetic granddaughter at Berry's expense," Jan fretted to her mother the next day while picking up Kimmie after school.

"I have an idea." Maria made sure Kimmie was busy playing with her dog Wiener before explaining. "Let me bring them both home with me for a sleepover after Thanksgiving dinner. That way I won't miss your dad and our traditions so much. And it's only fair for Berry to gain another grandma."

Jan hugged her. "I love you, Mom."

"I love you, too, *mija*." When they separated, her mother asked, "By the way, how are they getting along at home? They do fine here, but I keep them busy helping me." She'd babysat both girls a few times.

"They squabble occasionally, just like any pair of sisters. Mostly they're fine." The initial antagonism had vanished, to Jan's relief.

On Halloween, the pair had cavorted from house to house in their cat costumes. They collected thirty-seven dollars for the shelter, plus a twenty-dollar donation from Jan and Zack. Since then, they'd put their heads together with friends at school to dream up additional ways to raise money. Brady's mother, Kate, and Fiona's stepmom, Patty, seemed happy to take charge of that effort, so Jan left it to them.

She'd also been glad to resolve the financial issue with her former landlord. He was able to repair her apartment by cleaning rather than replacing the carpets, plus repainting the living room. He charged her half the six-hundred-dollar total, far less than she'd feared.

With that matter squared away, Jan continued to scan ads for a new home. December was rapidly approaching and she'd promised to get settled by Christmas. But her heart wasn't in it.

*I have to be tougher with myself,* she reflected. Right after the holiday, she vowed to search in earnest.

As the weeks flew by the protocols for the egg-donor program also began taking shape. On the Monday before Thanksgiving Jan devoted most of the afternoon to working with Dr. Samantha Forrest on how to present the risks to potential donors.

"Statistically, we're bound to have some young women run into problems," the pediatrician warned. They sat in a fifth-floor conference room, where the broad table provided room to spread out brochures and forms they'd collected from other similar programs. "It's important we not mislead anyone by soft-peddling this."

"No question—we agree on that." Jan leaned back, weary from two hours of discussing the common side effects of fertility drugs, which included abdominal swelling and mood swings, as well as rarer risks from both the medications and the process of egg retrieval, which involved sedation and minor surgery. "Don't forget the list of possible complications from taking aspirin can scare the wits out of you."

"All the same, people should be fully informed." Dr. Sam stretched. She'd been a little testy but at least willing to compromise. Although initially she'd insisted on a large disclaimer at the top of the donor materials, broadcasting the worst of the potential complications, after discussion, she'd agreed to start with a general warning that treatment carried possible serious side effects. These would be detailed later, following a description of the entire donation process.

Jan closed the file in her laptop. "I'll put together a draft. Then you and I, and other staff members, can give this a thorough review." Having concluded that business, she moved to a lighter topic. "How're your plans going for Thanksgiving?"

The blonde doctor fiddled with a pamphlet. "We'll have a full house. My parents are coming from Mexico, where they run a clinic, and Mark's sister plans to drive in from Arizona."

"Sounds like fun."

"With the triplets around, chaos is more like it. But I like being busy." Sam tapped the tabletop.

"Something bothering you?"

The pediatrician nodded unhappily. "I just learned this morning that the volunteer director of the counseling center is stepping down. Eleanor's a powerhouse. Without her direction and fund-raising, I don't see how we can continue."

"That's a shame." Although this development might give Zack's grant proposal a stronger chance of being endorsed by whoever won the contest, Jan hated to see the center go under.

"Maybe I'm too much of an idealist." Sam's mouth twisted. "I worry about the people who fall between the cracks, especially women and teenagers. Peer counselors can do so much good." She'd mentioned previously that many of the clients suffered from moderate depression or troubled relationships, or both.

"Why is your director leaving?" Jan asked.

"She's discouraged. Eleanor knocked herself out trying to raise funds among her wealthy friends but there are too many competing causes, especially in a tough economy. Yet I can't bear to let it go."

Even during her short time in Safe Harbor, Jan had heard a lot about the counseling center. She'd hate to see the community lose such a valuable resource, especially in a time of high unemployment and increased stress.

"Have you drawn up a business plan?" That seemed basic to Jan, but from what she'd heard, the center operated by the seat of its pants.

"Why?"

"To put the clinic's future into clearer focus. Also, you'll need one to attract corporate sponsorship."

Sam shook her head. "I wouldn't know where to start."

"You can find articles and templates on the internet," Jan said. "I'm sure there are some for volunteer organizations."

"The whole idea of the center is to keep things casual."

"That doesn't have to change," she assured the other woman. "Do you have a mission statement?"

"I think so." Sam looked uncertain. "We want to help people."

"Which people, and how do you plan to help them? Plus you should draw up a market analysis. Where does the center fit in among other agencies that serve a similar clientele?" Ideas flowed through Jan.

Dr. Sam jotted notes. "There's a lot to consider."

Perhaps because of her own impulsive nature, Jan had been impressed by the idea of business plans when she took courses in administration. "How big an endowment do you need? What kind of operating expenses do you foresee? Do you have a board of directors?"

"Not formally," Samantha conceded.

"Think about prominent people in the community who might serve on one," Jan pressed, gaining enthusiasm as she continued. "If you put it all in writing, you'll have a better picture of where you stand."

"Eleanor should like that." Sam made notes in her electronic tablet. "I'll talk to her. But I'm afraid she doesn't know about this stuff, either."

"If you have any questions, just call."

"Seriously?"

*How far am I willing to go with this?* Jan didn't mean to set herself up against Zack in the competition for the prize money. But that wasn't the issue here—for the center to survive, it had to get on a more professional footing. "I'll be glad to do what I can."

"Thank you." The pediatrician sprang to her feet. "I appreciate this." Collecting her gear, Samantha shook hands and took off at her usual top speed.

As Jan gathered her materials she felt a twinge of concern about how this might appear to Zack. But it wasn't a family matter. As long as she was doing the right thing, he had to respect her decisions.

Besides, with Thanksgiving only days away, Jan had more important, personal things to think about. Putting the incident out of her mind, she began stacking the materials to carry back to her office.

# Chapter Fifteen

Several years ago Zack had bought a good-quality camera to capture special moments with Berry. He wanted his daughter to cherish her memories of holidays and school events in sharp detail. Sometimes he forgot to bring it, however. At other times, he snapped a few shots then tucked the device away. Taking pictures felt like a duty, important but secondary. What mattered more was to experience one's life.

While that priority hadn't changed, on Thanksgiving he was glad to spend time behind the lens. Taking pictures gave him an excuse to move about freely and to observe with a fresh eye. And it might help make up for the lack of pictures at key moments in the past.

He'd always relished savory cooking scents and delicious food. Today, not only was it fun preparing the dishes with the girls and Jan, but as he snapped pictures, Zack appreciated the contrasting green and red of the lettuce and tomato salad, the glistening brown skin of the roasted turkey, and the dark red richness of the cranberry sauce.

What jumped out at him most, though, were the happy faces of the people he loved. Berry hadn't sparkled like this since her mother died, while Kimmie brimmed with high spirits. Jan seemed bathed in a glow as she moved from the kitchen to the dining room, where they'd added several card tables and covered the whole stretch with a couple of cloths.

As the guests trickled in, images became fixed in Zack's mind, so that later he was never sure whether he was remembering the reality or the photograph. Maria Garcia, gathering both little girls into an embrace. Jan's dark-haired brother, Bernardo, and his red-haired wife, Ginger, arms draped around middle-school daughters who'd been toddlers when Zack last saw them. Rima's brother, Edgar Williams, and his charming new girlfriend, a hairstylist, setting a mouthwatering sweet-potato casserole on the table. Edgar, a plumber, explained he'd met Alicia while replacing the pipes in her house.

Zack's parents arrived promptly at four o'clock, their expressions faintly disapproving when they discovered others had preceded them. Zack hoped they hadn't parked and waited, adhering to the old rule about not coming early to a dinner party.

The Sargents brought pies, along with toy penguins in Pilgrim clothing for the girls. Equal gifts, he was pleased to note. He'd mentioned in an email how much Berry loved the new doll. They'd apparently taken the hint.

For the meal, Zack set the camera aside. His parents seemed confused at first by the Garcia tradition of holding hands around the table, but they joined willingly in the prayer of thanks. Afterward, no one needed encouragement to pass the food.

When Zack's dad received Maria's plate of tamales, he regarded it with faint distaste. He was about to give it untouched to Bernardo when the younger man said, "I tell my history students Thanksgiving was a truly multicultural holiday, right from the start."

"You're a teacher?" No doubt unwilling to put himself in a bad light with a fellow educator, Norbert took a tamale.

"My wife, too." In his mid-thirties, Bernardo had a slightly receding hairline that added to his distinguished appearance. "I understand you're a retired principal."

"Before that I taught history, too." The men began discussing recent changes in the state's curriculum. Later, Zack noticed, his father not only finished the tamale but took a second.

As for the girls, Kimmie's cousins volunteered that they had two dogs and a cat, so Berry and Kimmie chattered about fund-raising for the shelter. After dinner, the four girls trooped upstairs to play with the cats, a scene Zack felt privileged to witness. Ordinarily, he wouldn't have intruded, but with camera in hand he became part of the fun.

Still, the center of the day was Jan. Photographing her chatting with Alicia, helping one of her nieces retie a hair ribbon or sharing a warm conversation with her mother, he noticed how naturally she brought people together. He even caught his mother giving her a rare hug. Although Norbert kept his distance at first, he unwound enough later to put on an apron and wash pots with Jan.

"Bert's unhappy she kept Kimmie away from you and us," Zack's mom confided to him. "On the other hand, he's glad she didn't give her up for adoption."

"What's with the apron thing?" Zack asked. "I never saw Dad do dishes before."

"He's mellowed in retirement," his mother responded.

"I'm sure you had something to do with that." To the rest of the world Elspeth Sargent might appear meek, but her son recognized the steel in her spine.

"I informed him that since he's retired and I'm not, it's

only fair for him to work around the house," his mother said. "I let him choose which chores he minds least."

"Washing pots and pans?"

"He's good with a vacuum, too." She smiled, looking younger than she had in years.

Not only were old acquaintances renewed, but Zack saw new connections forming. After dinner, while many of the guests gathered in the den to watch a football game, Jan and Edgar stood talking quietly in the living room in front of a framed photo of Rima. They didn't seem to notice Zack standing in the doorway, capturing the two of them with his late wife in the background. As he studied them through the lens, it felt as if they were all three present.

"Heart trouble runs in our family," he heard Edgar say. "I'm all about exercise and healthy eating. Might have some of that pie, though."

"I guess that's why Zack is so strict about Berry's diet," Jan replied.

"Couldn't ask for a better dad for my niece." At six foot two, Edgar towered over Jan, but his soft-spoken manner obviously put her at ease. "Wish I'd been around more for my big sis. Being in the Marines, I was gone a lot."

"I wish I'd known her." Catching sight of Zack, Jan addressed her next remark to him. "You must have taken a hundred pictures today."

"Fortunately, I have a big SIM card," he replied cheerfully. "It can hold a lot more than that."

"Post those on Facebook?" Edgar asked.

"You bet."

Zack moved to Jan's side. Until now, he'd avoided any indication they were a couple, aware that their families must be curious. Yet he missed touching her, being close, catching the scent of her hair. Keeping his distance was becoming harder by the minute.

"Guess I'd better see who's winning that game," Edgar said without further discussion, and ambled toward the den.

"I didn't mean to drive him away." Zack switched off the camera. Was his desire to be alone with Jan that obvious?

She moved closer. "Thank you for today." Her face tilted up toward his.

"Why are you thanking me?" Too bad there wasn't a Thanksgiving equivalent of mistletoe to give him an excuse to kiss her. *As if anyone would believe it.*

"I can be kind of a bulldozer when I seize on an idea." She stroked his arm lightly. "You're a good sport about hosting all these people."

"You think this is a hardship?" Zack tapped her nose with his finger. "It's the best Thanksgiving in years."

Standing so close, he noticed how her pearl earrings nestled into her lobes, inviting him to nibble. Loose curls added a wild, bedroom quality to her usually tame hair. As for her mouth, the full lips parted invitingly when he gazed at them.

Outside, a car spun down the street too fast, braking with a screech at the corner. Jolted to awareness, Jan took a step back and broke eye contact.

Zack didn't want her to go yet. He ached for more of this tantalizing closeness. More temptation. And perhaps just a little yielding.

Jan indicated Rima's picture. "You must miss her, especially during the holidays."

The reference to his late wife brought Zack down to earth, as no doubt Jan intended. It also reminded him of something he'd been meaning to explain. His engagement to Rima had destroyed any chance of reconciling with Jan, and she deserved to understand what had happened.

While he would never be disloyal to Rima's memory, it troubled him to see the old hurt, a reminder of the abandonment Jan must have felt. He'd become engaged before he learned she'd been falsely accused, but even when he did, he'd gone ahead with the marriage and left her to have the baby without him. "She meant a lot to me," he began.

"We should get back to our guests."

"Not yet." He caught her hand and let the words pour out. "Rima was a heart patient at the hospital when I met her. She'd lost her job as a salesclerk because she couldn't stand on her feet all day, and her insurance was running out. On top of that, she had trouble keeping up with an active toddler. Social Services was threatening to put Berry in a foster home."

Jan caught her breath. "How horrible. Weren't there any other relatives?"

"Rima's parents were dead and Berry's father had died in a motorcycle accident a year earlier." Not wanting to make Rima sound like a charity case, Zack hurried on. "I was miserable and depressed. I still loved you but I felt betrayed. On top of that, I had bad dreams about giving up our daughter. I'm not making excuses for the way I behaved toward you. It's just that Rima and Berry filled a big hole in my heart."

Although a deep breath shivered through Jan, she didn't pull away. "And you fell in love with her."

"She became an important part of my life very fast." Zack didn't know how else to respond. Yes, he'd come to love Rima, but not with the same intensity, the same sense of belonging he'd experienced with Jan. Only he could never say that, because if he did, he risked Berry finding out. "Jan, when I asked her to marry me, she lit up with excitement. It was as if I'd handed her the whole world. A future for herself and her daughter."

"And you couldn't have backed out even if you'd wanted to," she finished for him.

He cupped her face with his hand. Oh, how badly he wanted to kiss her—for understanding, and for simply being here. "I felt you should know."

"It helps." In her eyes he saw a ragged flash of regret. "It always bothered me you got over me so fast. Like it hadn't been real."

"It was." He couldn't go beyond that, not yet. But he was beginning to wonder if this rift might be mendable, after all.

The thump and clatter of the girls swarming down the staircase drew their attention to the hall. He stepped back quickly.

"Can we have dessert now, Aunt Jan?" asked her thirteen-year-old niece, coming into view.

"Sure," Jan replied. "Let's start slicing the pies."

Berry lingered as the others trooped off. "Daddy?"

As a rule, Zack banned sweets. Today was different. "Honey, it's a holiday. Of course you can have pie."

She gave a little hop of joy. "Thanks!" Then she paused in deep concentration. "Which one should I have?"

There was a selection of apple, pumpkin and cherry. "Which do you like best?"

"I don't know."

As Berry clasped her hands, Zack noticed the similarities to Rima's photo: the oval face, dark winged eyebrows, brown hair frizzing in ringlets. The intelligence and the vulnerability. "How about a thin slice of each?"

"Really?" She stared at him in amazement. "I can do that?"

"You bet."

When she flung her arms around him, it was like their first meeting all over again. An urgent desire to protect her swept over Zack.

"Yay!" With that happy cry, she scampered off. It was the most heartfelt statement of thanksgiving he'd heard all day.

*He never stopped loving me.* Zack hadn't dismissed Jan from his heart and replaced her with someone who truly belonged there. Instead, he'd met a lovely woman with a sweet little girl and taken them under his wing. By the time he learned the truth about the accusations, he'd been too involved to leave them. How could he have done otherwise?

As Jan watched Zack slide thin slices of pie onto Berry's plate and then do the same for Kimmie, her heart swelled with a yearning so poignant it hurt. Did he have to be so endearing, grinning sideways at her? Did his laughter have to rumble through her body, setting off a cascade of fireworks? Did he have to sound so earnest and caring, in response to a question about his work at the hospital, when he described his dream of setting up a grant program for patients?

When he mentioned the Hope Challenge, Kimmie listened intently. Through a bite of pie, she spluttered, "You could win a humble mumble dollars?"

"Don't talk with your mouth full," her older cousin responded.

Kimmie puffed out her cheeks defiantly. Jan was glad to see the protest went no further.

"You could do a lot of good with that much money," Zack's father remarked. "My only regret in working at a private school was that we had a limited number of scholarships."

"How wonderful to help families who can't afford treatment," Alicia said.

Kimmie swallowed her pie and plunged in again. "What about the animal shelter?"

"I'll bet there are a lot of charities that could use that kind of money," Jan's sister-in-law, Ginger, pointed out.

"True. We have some heated competition." Zack explained the rivalry with the counseling center, adding, "The latest word is that its volunteer director may be leaving. I'd hate to see the program fold. On the other hand…"

"All volunteer projects reach a point where they either have to become professional or they fall apart," Bernardo observed.

"Too bad if they got all that money and it went down the drain," Edgar agreed.

"Glad I have your support. Now if you guys will run out and get pregnant for me, I'll be a shoo-in." Chuckling, Zack began collecting dishes. "Who'll help wash up?"

"Me!"

"Me!" Kimmie and Berry were on their feet, with the older girls following suit. Soon they'd whisked away the plates and the kitchen echoed with the sounds of running water, clinking china and high-pitched voices.

Afterward, some of the guests resumed watching football and others moved the card tables into the living room to play dominoes and Monopoly. Jan reveled in the high spirits and sense of harmony.

The girls gravitated to Zack, playing a board game that involved launching figures through the air and laughing uproariously. He clowned around while ensuring each girl got her turn.

He was such a good man. If they tried again, could it work this time?

Jan was almost afraid to hope—but she couldn't help it.

## Chapter Sixteen

By nine o'clock the last of the guests had departed. Kimmie and Berry, who'd packed their overnight bags in advance, gave the cats a cuddle and trotted off happily with Maria.

Jan was delighted at how well the families had blended. Zack's father had spent over an hour discussing educational issues with Bernardo and Ginger, while Alicia and Edgar had played a rousing bridge game with Maria and Zack's mother. Jan had never seen Elspeth Sargent so animated.

Throughout the evening she sensed Zack's attention skimming over her, no matter what else he was doing. Their eyes would meet, and then he'd go back to refilling glasses, joking with the girls or watching a recap of the day's football highlights.

Her skin prickled with excitement. They were going to be alone tonight. She knew what that might mean, and judging by the quick intake of his breath whenever they came close, so did he.

Ever since she'd seen Zack standing in front of the third-grade classroom a couple of months ago, Jan had longed to touch him all over. She couldn't stop now, even though her instincts warned she'd be running a risk. If this relationship blew up in their faces, their delicate balance over Kimmie's upbringing might shatter.

*No matter how much caution I've learned, I'm still impulsive.* And this particular impulse refused to be ignored.

They circulated in the empty house, collecting a forgotten glass here, a dropped crumb there. Repositioning chairs, realigning a table runner. When Zack reached for a misplaced candy dish and his wrist brushed Jan's arm, the fleeting contact felt so intense she flushed.

"Jan," Zack murmured, facing her in the den. He smelled of soap, wood and a hint of pumpkin.

Jan drank in the familiar sight of dark blond hair falling across his forehead, and skin golden despite the lateness of the season. She lifted her arms to drape around his shoulders. "Yes?"

His palms slid around her waist and their lips met. Lightly. Softly. Jan stood on tiptoe, relearning the curve of his jaw and the pulse of his throat.

To her astonishment, she discovered he was trembling. "Zack?"

"Let's go upstairs."

He didn't have to suggest it twice.

Until now, Jan had glanced into the master bedroom but hadn't entered. She stepped inside shyly, taking in the bureau and entertainment center of golden oak, the brass bedstead and the royal-blue quilt. The furnishings melded masculinity with a sense of openness, much like the man Zack had become. But of course his wife must have chosen these.

When she hesitated, his hand came to rest on her back. "I bought these after I moved here," he said.

"It doesn't matter." But it did.

Then Zack drew her deeper into the room and Jan forgot everything else. When he cupped her face to kiss her, she lost herself in his tenderness. It seemed as if they'd both come home after a long journey.

Unworking the buttons on her pink cardigan, he murmured, "You wore this just to frustrate me, didn't you?"

"Shouldn't be much of a challenge for a surgeon," Jan teased back. "Those deft fingers..."

"Oh, you like those, do you?" He opened it to reveal her pink lace-edged bra. "You always had exquisite taste in lingerie."

"You remember?"

"You'd be surprised what I remember."

Aching to feel his skin, she lifted his green sweater. It stuck halfway up, baring his chest. Jan leaned forward and ran her tongue down the center.

Zack groaned. With an effort, he yanked the sweater over his head and tossed it aside. "Whoever invented clothes was an idiot."

"I hear they can be useful in cold climates," Jan murmured.

"Good thing we're in Southern California."

Her cardigan and beige wool skirt joined his slacks in a friendly heap on the floor. He used to fold everything neatly before making love, Jan recalled, half expecting him to take a moment to do so now.

"Aha." Zack flipped her onto the bed. "Caught you off guard."

"You used to..."

"Never mind that. I've grown up." He grinned. "Uh, hold that thought." He sprang to his feet, returning a moment later with a condom. "One surprise baby is a gift. Two might be considered careless."

"Especially in view of our professions."

He unwrapped the protection. As Jan helped slide it into place, she cherished the strength of him, the power and the vulnerability. Then they caressed each other, legs tangling on the bed, bodies arching together. When he held himself over her and bent down for a kiss, they merged like liquid silver.

Excitement rushed into her. For a moment, they held still, feeling the connection, scarcely daring to move. Then, with a gasp, Zack began to thrust. Joy flooded through Jan. All these years, without realizing it, she'd been waiting for him to come back.

As their rhythm grew wilder and more insistent, they soared from the earth, flying toward the sun and exploding in a great rapturous burst. Shudders vibrated through Zack and into Jan until, slowly, they glided to earth, landing light as a whisper.

She lay quietly satisfied. Zack tugged the covers over them and Jan nestled against his shoulder. The words "I love you" drifted out of her.

He didn't answer. Had he heard?

She shouldn't have spoken. It was too soon. And too late, because hard as Jan had fought not to give him her heart, she'd done it anyway.

*I LOVE YOU, TOO.* The words formed in Zack's mind but never reached his mouth.

He longed to lie here sharing endearments, suffused with the glory of their lovemaking. Yet if he said those words, everything would change. He wasn't ready for that. More importantly, Berry wasn't ready.

Zack had seen how easily her sense of security could be shaken. Although she'd adapted to their new housemates better than he'd expected, she'd done so with the awareness this was only temporary and that she came first with him. Moreover, if she ever suspected he hadn't loved her mother the way he loved Jan, she might believe he didn't love her as much as Kimmie. Although that wasn't true, she'd be devastated.

Maybe he should talk over his concern with Jan and assess how to deal with it together. But she'd gotten out of bed already and gone to the bathroom. Besides, speaking without thinking led to misunderstandings.

Zack sat up, his brain busy sorting out the ramifications of what had happened. No regrets, and he hoped she had none, either. But they needed to take things slowly. While making love had brought them closer, it hadn't resolved all their differences.

When Jan returned, Zack welcomed her back under the covers. "About what we did," he began.

"I'm not making any assumptions," she replied softly.

It hurt him to see a trace of sadness in her eyes. "It was wonderful. Please don't think…"

"It can't happen again. For now." Tension frayed her voice. "We have to set a good example for the girls. Is that what you mean?"

Not exactly, but she was on the right track. "It's best to take things slow." Could they become a family, the four of them? With room for Berry to feel completely loved and accepted?

"Okay. We'll play it by ear." Jan sat up, hugging her knees.

"Yes. What's the rush, anyway?" He stroked her hair across the velvety skin of her shoulders. In the lamplight, she had the burnished radiance of a Renaissance painting. "You're beautiful."

Jan touched his cheek. "So are you." Then she slid away and went to collect her clothes. "I'll sleep in my own room. If the girls get homesick, Mom might bring them home early."

Zack hadn't considered that. "You're right." Yet they'd

left too much unspoken. "Jan, we ought to…" He couldn't figure out how to finish the sentence.

"You think too much," she said, and whisked out of the room.

At least she was smiling.

THE GIRLS RETURNED THE next morning, bubbling about some project they'd dreamed up to help the animal shelter. "Can we go over to Brady's house?" Kimmie asked as soon as Maria drove off.

"What's going on?" Jan inquired, surprised the kids would be in a hurry to leave again so soon.

"It's a secret! Can we, please?"

"You shouldn't keep secrets from your parents," Zack responded gently.

"Not *that* kind of secret," Kimmie reproved. "Nothing bad."

"More like a surprise," Berry added. "A good one."

How wonderful the girls had united. "I don't see the harm." After glancing at Zack and catching his nod, Jan said, "I'll call Brady's mother. If it's okay with her, I'll take you there."

"I'd suggest we all do something together, but I have to work." Although most of the doctors were off the Friday after Thanksgiving, Zack had on-call duty.

He'd been right about last night, Jan reflected as she cleared the visit with Kate and got the girls ready to go. Making any obvious shift in their relationship at this point would upset the harmony they'd worked so hard to achieve. All the same, it stung that Zack hadn't said he loved her.

She wasn't sure what to do about finding a new place to live. So far, her search had turned up no suitable prospects. Since she and Zack had agreed in principle not to make a decision yet about their relationship, why bring up the subject? With the Christmas holidays approaching and their parenting in sync, it made sense to put off any decision until after the first of the year.

Although Jan wasn't crazy about leaving their living arrangement up in the air, she was too busy to give it much thought. Coordinating the girl's activities, setting up the egg bank's protocols, finalizing the brochure for prospective donors—everything took more time than she'd expected, including a meeting a week later with Dr. Forrest to review revisions to the brochure.

No sooner had they finished going over the changes suggested by other staff members than the pediatrician brought up the counseling center. "Eleanor doesn't have a head for business and I'm afraid I don't, either." Sam leaned back at the desk in her office. It was four-thirty on a Friday afternoon. Jan hoped to wrap this up quickly so she could put in an hour or so of Christmas shopping.

"You might consider hiring a consultant." She glanced at a photo on Sam's desk of the adopted triplets Courtney, Connie and Colin. Nearly two years old, the trio looked poised to burst out of the picture. Even with a full-time nanny, Sam and Mark must have their hands full.

Living up to her nickname of Fightin' Sam, the pediatrician gave Jan a determined stare. "You're the best expert I know."

"I'm not—"

The protest got cut off in midsentence. "I've already identified some counseling and support groups in the area so we can analyze what needs they *aren't* filling. That's what you suggested, right? Then I'll put Eleanor to work finding a board of directors and convincing them the community should support us."

Jan made one more attempt to wiggle free. "I can't really spare the time now. Perhaps later."

"Once the center closes, it's gone forever."

Sam was right. But what would Zack think? The timing, so close to the end of the contest, was extremely awkward. In a sense Jan would be helping his rival.

She winced. Was she seriously planning to abandon a worthy cause for fear of Zack's disapproval? She'd gone into nursing to help people, and into administration to make the best use of her organizational skills. That's what Sam was asking—for her to use those skills in the service of a good cause. "Well, let's see what we can come up with before I have to pick up my daughter."

"I knew I could count on you!" Energy and enthusiasm bubbled from Dr. Sam and spilled over onto Jan.

They worked longer than she'd expected, nearly two hours. By the end they'd roughed out an analysis and the gist of a mission statement. "I leave it to you and Eleanor to do the rest."

"Absolutely!" The pediatrician stretched her shoulders. "You've been fantastic."

"Thanks." Silently, Jan wondered if the facts and arguments they'd assembled would be enough to inspire patronage. In a tight economy and with churches taking up some of the slack left by pinched nonprofits, the center looked more and more like an exercise in good intentions. However, she refused to be negative. "I know you can pull this off."

"Especially if we get that prize money." Sam grinned.

"Right." Feeling guilty, Jan picked up her briefcase and hurried out.

Should she mention the consultation to Zack? She intended to, but not tonight, not when she was so tired.

And not the next night, or the one after that. Whenever

the two of them found rare moments alone, Jan hated to spoil the mood. Soothing him, making him laugh, winning a look of tenderness as he gazed at her—those things made her happy. As for the rapidly approaching conclusion of the Hope Challenge, it was creating more than enough tension already.

To increase the suspense, the administration had quit posting the relative positions of the competitors. That didn't stop doctors from calculating their odds or the staff from conjecturing. With Zack's freshly honed surgical skills and growing patient load, his rate of pregnancies inched upward, while Dr. Tartikoff's recent decision to spend more time with his family was rumored to have a leveling effect on his successes. As for Dr. Rayburn, public opinion—which reached Jan via Caroline's hard-to-miss chitchat in the outer office—held that he ought to withdraw because of his position as hospital administrator.

The secretary's addiction to gossip remained both an annoyance and, occasionally, a source of information. Since Jan hadn't detected her accessing the internet during work hours, she refrained from rebuking the chirpy young woman.

"Did you hear the latest?" Caroline demanded on the Monday before the scheduled big announcement. "Dr. Forrest was all set to close her counseling center but now she and that volunteer, what's-her-name, have come up with a plan to save it!"

Jan's stomach churned on the lunch she'd just finished eating. She was pleased, yet troubled, too, although she hadn't done anything wrong. "I wish them luck."

"I'll bet Dr. Sargent won't be happy." Caroline fixed her gaze on Jan, watching for her reaction. The secretary had been angling for details about their living arrangement, making offhand references Jan ignored.

"He and Dr. Forrest both care about the community," Jan said. "They're just focused on different projects."

"I guess you know him better than anyone." Receiving no response, Caroline continued. "Didn't you say you'd be moving out after Thanksgiving?"

Jan hadn't mentioned that to the secretary, but she might have said something to Melissa or Karen within earshot. "I haven't found the right place yet."

"They have to take pets, right?" The young woman bounced in her seat. "Well, I've got a solution! There's this house down the street from us. The renters moved out a few days ago and they had a couple of dogs. Mom says it hasn't been advertised because they left it a mess."

Jan bit off the acid comment that living near Caroline disqualified the place immediately. That would be rude. "If it isn't available…"

"The owners live next door to us." The secretary shared a house with her parents. "I bet they'd be glad to show it to you. I mean, they'd save the cost of advertising, right? And we could vouch for you."

"Any idea what it rents for?"

"Sorry, no."

Had this been anyone else, Jan would have put her off. But she and Zack had stuck to the story that, following her unexpected loss of the apartment, he'd agreed to let her move in for Kimmie's sake. They'd avoided driving to work together or giving any other sign of functioning as a couple.

Making excuses not to view the house would only fuel Caroline's rumor mill. Besides, given the mess, perhaps the owners had changed their minds about allowing pets. And the rent might be too high. "I'd be happy to take a look," Jan said. "Do you have the owners' phone number?"

"I'll text it to you right now." Whipping out her phone, Caroline tapped the buttons.

"Thanks." Jan went into her office. Seriously, what harm could it do to check the place out?

*It could do a lot of harm if Caroline reports on every move I make.* Jan wondered reluctantly whether she ought to have the secretary transferred to another office. Her nosiness was inappropriate and bothersome.

Glancing down, Jan read the text message on her phone. Then, she unwillingly put in a call to the landlord.

## Chapter Seventeen

On Thursday, the day before the announcement for the Hope Challenge winner, Zack struggled to keep that awareness from affecting his mood. The discovery that some staff members were taking bets didn't help, nor did overhearing that several bloggers were discussing the pros and cons of his versus Samantha's proposals.

The pediatrician had a talent for drawing media interest. A comment on her Facebook account about how she and Eleanor Wycliff were crafting a business plan even sparked a small item in the local newspaper. Will Help Center Live or Die? read a headline on page three.

A business plan. Dr. Sam should have thought of that a long time ago. Why did she have to come up with it now?

During the morning, he kept busy with surgeries and, later, with patient appointments. Just as he was about to finish dictating his reports for the day, he was called next door to the hospital to admit a fertility patient. Only six weeks into her pregnancy, she'd suffered a miscarriage.

In her early forties, the woman had a child from a previous marriage but had been trying for five years to have another. At this age, the odds were against her.

After examining her, Zack sat with the patient and her husband. He gave them the facts: 15 to 20 percent of all known pregnancies resulted in miscarriage, and the cause was likely to be a chromosomal abnormality, for which her blood was being tested. If that was the case, nothing could have prevented this loss.

That didn't make it any less heartbreaking.

A few minutes later, as he passed the nurses' station, a young aide remarked cheerily it was a good thing miscarriages didn't affect the pregnancy rate for the contest. Zack rounded on her furiously. "Don't be so insensitive! What if the patient heard?"

Tears sprang to her eyes. "I'm sorry, doctor."

He felt bad for lashing out even though she *had* been out of line. Still, the best he could manage was to add, "We need to keep in mind that we're in a caring profession."

"Yes, doctor."

As he turned away, the devastation on her face made Zack feel even worse. But whatever else he might say was likely to sound like a further rebuke, so he let it go.

Usually, if he was running late, Jan picked up Berry at her sitter's. Today she'd informed him she had to catch up on some errands before collecting Kimmie, and it was nearly seven by the time they both arrived home, each with a daughter in tow. Despite Zack's effort to buy healthy fast food, the chicken tasted greasy and the salad dressing turned out to be regular instead of low-fat.

After dinner he performed deep-breathing exercises to restore his perspective. No sense taking out his irritability on the others. Still, it was a relief when the girls went to bed and he could retreat to the den to catch up on his medical journals.

When Jan sat beside him on the couch, Zack noted rebellious wisps of hair curling around her face. She must have had a rough day, too. Then he caught the faint smell of—was that dog? No wonder Gorilla had hissed at her earlier.

"Do you have a minute?" she asked. "I'd like to show you something."

"Sure." He set aside the tablet on which he'd been reading. "What's up?"

She held out her phone, displaying a snapshot of a small ranch-style house. "The reason I was late was that I went to see this rental. The owner's willing to allow pets and the price is reasonable. It's only a mile from here."

"You're planning to move?" He thought they'd agreed to play this by ear.

She set down the phone. "Caroline suggested this place. She knows the owners. I could hardly refuse to look."

"And now you can't find a good reason to turn it down?" he responded edgily.

"That's why I'm showing it to you!" Her temper flared, as well. "If Kimmie and I are moving I'd like to get settled before Christmas, and this place meets my specifications. Or it will when it's cleaned. Once it's advertised it won't last more than a few days, so I have to decide quickly."

"How quickly?" he grumbled.

"By Sunday."

Zack nearly blurted, "Turn it down." But then what? There'd be no guarantee of finding another suitable place next month. If he insisted she stay, he ought to make a commitment at least until the end of the school year. Given the hospital grapevine, that practically amounted to a public declaration of their involvement.

He wanted to keep on waking up in the same house, hearing Jan's voice in the morning and inhaling the scent of her shampoo. Sharing meals, seeing how smoothly she corralled the girls for school and at bedtime. Talking things over with her. Enjoying the merriment on her face when they kidded around, the rush of warmth whenever she brushed against him. And for weeks he'd been longing to arrange another night alone.

He couldn't decide what step to take next. Not in his current mood. After tomorrow, no matter how the contest turned out, the pressure would be off and the two of them could discuss the future more sensibly.

"Hold off till the weekend, will you?" Zack asked.

She glanced down at the picture. "Okay. Do I smell like dog?"

"A little."

"The place reeked of it." She clicked off the phone.

Curiosity pricked him. "When did you learn about this place?"

"Monday." Catching his startled expression, she said, "I didn't want to say anything with the girls around. I kept putting it off and it slipped my mind."

No sense getting snarly over a minor omission. "It's okay. But, Jan, no more surprises, please."

"I promise." She leaned against him. "By the way, the girls are out of school tomorrow. It's one of those teacher prep days. Kate volunteered to watch them and I thought that would be okay."

"She's been very helpful," Zack said. "We should return the favor."

"Good idea. I'm sure she and Tony would enjoy a night out."

As she snuggled against him it occurred to Zack that until Jan moved in, he'd kept track of the school's schedule himself. He'd come to depend on her more than he'd realized.

They functioned well together. He didn't like to think about her moving out—not at all.

THE STAFF GATHERING WAS set for noon on Friday. The press
and those who couldn't attend could follow the proceed-
ings via a live internet feed on the hospital's website.

That morning in her office Jan tried to review the latest state regulations affecting her program, but her mind
kept drifting to last night. Zack had seemed displeased
at the idea of her leaving. Afterward, they'd read side by
side on the couch in companionable silence. He hadn't
asked her to stay, though. Perhaps it was time for a serious discussion.

*Long overdue, really.* She disliked bringing up touchy
issues, but avoiding them didn't make them go away.

They also needed to compare notes about the girls,
who'd become increasingly secretive. This morning Jan
had meant to drive them to Kate's house, to ask Brady's
mom straight out what the children were planning. Then
Zack had offered to play chauffeur, to Berry and Kimmie's delight. Unable to speak frankly in front of them,
Jan had suggested he have a friendly chat with Kate, and
hoped he'd taken the hint.

She emerged from her office at a quarter to twelve.
Caroline had called in sick, while Cole, Melissa and Karen
had already left for the auditorium. When the outer door
opened and she spotted Zack, Jan's spirits rose at the idea
he might want to sit with her in public.

Then she registered his scowl. "What's wrong?"

He glanced around before answering sharply, "I
thought we'd agreed, no more surprises."

Jan searched her mind in vain. The morning had gone
smoothly, as far as she could tell. "What do you mean?"

"When I dropped the kids off, Kate mentioned how
kind it was of you to help Dr. Forrest save her program."
Zack gestured in frustration. "You're the one who pro-

posed the business plan. And from what I've heard, practically drew it up single-handedly."

"That's not true!" Well, not entirely. "Sam was helping with the brochure for donors and we got to talking about the center. I do have a background in business. I couldn't refuse to help just because it's inconvenient for you."

"And you saw no reason to mention this to me?" His low tone brimmed with anger.

"I just…" Jan stopped. Why was she on the defensive? "It's a worthwhile project, even if it is competing with yours."

"Every time I start to relax and feel like I can trust you, I get blindsided." How well she remembered that judgmental tone.

"Not everything in the world is about you!" Jan shot back.

"I see." Arms folded, Zack waited sternly. For her to apologize?

It was on the tip of Jan's tongue to do that, but it felt wrong. She *wasn't* sorry she'd helped Dr. Sam. "Isn't it time we went to the meeting?"

"Yes, but…" Zack shook his head. "Nora Franco, who happens to be Kate's sister-in-law, just asked me if it's true you're backing the counseling center over my grant project. You've made me feel like an idiot and embarrassed me in front of my colleagues."

"That's not fair!"

"Not from your perspective, obviously. Oh, what's the use?" He swung around and stalked out.

Jan held back. It would kindle even more speculation if they walked in together with tension snapping between them. Besides, she needed to marshal her thoughts.

She understood his project meant a lot, and that her aiding the competition might feel disloyal. But was this how it would always be—Zack quick to assign blame, Jan questioning her values and perhaps even suppressing her instincts for fear of provoking him?

That wasn't her idea of a healthy relationship. And she disliked the prospect of Kimmie growing up believing a woman ought to clip her wings to maintain peace with a man.

It hurt to think of leaving. Once she did that, they might never be truly close again. But no matter how much she loved Zack, putting distance between them might be the best thing.

Her heart twisting, Jan hurried to the auditorium.

As Zack took a seat in the nearly full hall, he supposed he should have saved his confrontation with Jan for later when they'd have more time. There was nothing he could do to change that now. As it was, he'd been one of the last to arrive at this critical event.

Colleagues from the administrative and medical staff filled the tiered rows of seats in the wood-paneled room. On the stage Dr. T sat between Mark Rayburn and Chandra Yashimoto, vice-president of Medical Center Management Inc. Straight dark hair fell in a sharp slash just above the collar of her lavender wool suit. On the floor, her designer briefcase presumably held a symbolic check for a hundred thousand dollars.

Zack's fists tightened. He hated to think of so much money being wasted on a program that wasn't likely to survive, no matter how many pie charts and rosy forecasts Jan and Samantha created. Meanwhile, he'd had two patients this week decline fertility treatments because insurance didn't cover them.

Jan should have known better than to encourage Sa-

mantha. More importantly, she'd promised no more secrets between them, all the while keeping this one.

The buzz of voices died as Mark took the podium. The
administrator exuded a natural leadership Zack admired
and wished he could emulate. Even after three years at
Safe Harbor, he still felt like the new kid around here.

"Welcome to the grand finale of the Hope Challenge."
Dr. Rayburn went on to describe the nature of the competition, the prize and the significant growth in the pregnancy rate achieved during the past nine months. Zack
assumed this information, well-known to the staff, was
primarily for the benefit of the press and public on the
internet.

"Now for my first announcement," Mark continued.
"There's been some heated advocacy for a couple of charity proposals. I think it's best for everyone if I remain neutral. Therefore I'm taking myself out of the competition
and turning the meeting over to the head of our fertility
program, Dr. Owen Tartikoff."

Zack released a low sigh of relief. Not that the removal
of one leading contender guaranteed anything, but it didn't
hurt.

The russet-haired fertility director sprang up, shook
Mark's hand and claimed the podium. "Hey, it's great
being up here. I love an audience. How's everybody feeling today?"

"Oh, get on with it," demanded a male voice from the
audience. Dr. Rod Vintner was one of the few staffers bold
enough to take an occasional poke at the powers that be.
Also, as an anesthesiologist, he had no stake in the results.

"Hecklers will be shot, but okay," Owen responded
with a good-natured grin. "Now, as you're all aware, I've
been the front-runner for most of the challenge, but the
gap has been narrowing. Also, my toughest critic—that

would be my wife, Bailey—informs me I'm being unfair. First, my practice is limited to fertility patients, unlike most of yours. Second, although it was under my supervision, Dr. Zack Sargent actually performed some of the surgeries that led to pregnancies for which I got credit. So, like Mark, I'm withdrawing."

Murmurs rippled through the crowd. Zack could hardly swallow. Could he have won, after all? From the row below him, Paige and Nora gave him thumbs-up signs.

"And since we've established the principle that some conceptions can be credited to more than one doctor, that bumps Zack up in the ratings. Now, without further ado…" Dr. T. paused for dramatic effect. "The winner of the Hope Challenge is…Dr. Cole Rattigan."

Sporadic applause greeted this announcement, along with some puzzled whispering. No one knew which charity the new head of the men's fertility program favored. As for Zack, it took him a moment to accept that after the lift he'd felt on learning about the additional credits, he'd lost nevertheless.

Or had he? Striding up to the podium amid belated applause, the urologist looked a bit dazed. Most likely he'd seen this contest as a game. Now he had to consider how seriously the rest of the staff took the results.

He might choose to endow the grant program. That was what really mattered.

"Wow." After shaking hands with Dr. T, the brown-haired newcomer gazed across the auditorium. "This is quite an honor."

"Honor shmonor!" Rod proclaimed from the back row. "Who gets the moolah?" Nervous laughter greeted this crack.

"There are several worthy proposals," Cole said. "But

even though Dr. Rayburn stepped down, he was ahead of me. So I'm going to designate his wife's program."

Zack sat in stunned silence, along with most of the staff. The grant project had lost. While Zack had already resolved to seek other means of support, without an initial infusion of money it was likely to be a long, hard road.

"Hang on!" In the row behind Zack, Samantha Forrest sprang to her feet. Tall and forceful, she had no trouble projecting her voice to fill the room. "I have some news of my own."

He hoped she wasn't going to brag about her center, now that she'd won, Zack reflected in annoyance. Not that he begrudged her a future for her program. He just wished both projects could succeed.

"If I'd had any idea how exciting it was to work at Safe Harbor, I'd have joined the staff sooner," Cole answered. "Care to come up here?"

"No," Sam said. "Can everybody hear me?"

"Eh?" Rod cupped his ear teasingly.

"We can hear you fine," Mark called from the stage.

"Okay, then." Sam cleared her throat. "With tremendous help from Jan Garcia and Eleanor Wycliff, I drew up a business plan. The goal was to put the counseling center on a firm basis with an endowment and a paid director. But after we ran the numbers, I had to admit a hundred thousand dollars would be a drop in the bucket."

"You could raise more from the community," said childbirth educator Tina Torres, sitting to one side.

"I'm afraid that's an overly rosy assumption. Eleanor made a few calls, and frankly, the response was dismal." Sam took a deep breath. "I've concluded the grant program Zack has proposed for fertility patients will not only prove self-sustaining but will grow, whereas the counseling center simply isn't viable in the long term."

"And you just came to that conclusion this very minute?" Rod asked.

"I'd have announced it earlier, but Mark said I should hold off," Sam replied. "A little drama never hurts. Anyway, since we're losing our current quarters as of January first, we'll be closing the counseling program this month. I'd like to thank all those who've worked on our behalf."

Sympathetic comments greeted her declaration. Zack's stomach tightened. It looked as if he'd won, but he hadn't wanted it to happen this way.

From the corner of his eye, he glimpsed Jan standing amid the overflow attendees. Ironically, her suggestion had apparently contributed to Samantha's coming to terms with reality.

Or perhaps not so ironically. Zack hadn't seen the whole picture. He wished he hadn't vented his frustration on Jan.

Sam resumed her seat next to the hospital publicity director, Jennifer Serra Martin. Although the center had been established in honor of Jennifer's infant son, who had died many years ago, she appeared to be taking this news in stride. No doubt Sam had alerted her in advance.

"Well…" Cole cleared his throat, and all attention was riveted on him again.

Zack's teeth hurt from clenching them. Despite Sam's withdrawal, Cole could choose any charity he wished. There were plenty of worthy organizations.

But Dr. T was back on his feet. "Oh, that reminds me." He did love throwing a monkey wrench into things. "There's one more charity whose advocates have asked to be heard."

"You've got to be kidding." Zack didn't realize he'd spoken aloud until faces turned toward him. His cheeks burned.

"I'm sure Dr. Sargent won't object when he sees who it is." Owen indicated the rear of the auditorium, where his wife had appeared. Bailey was smiling so broadly even her freckles seemed to twinkle. "Why don't you show them in?"

Puzzled, Zack craned for a better view as the doors opened. He heard people say, "How cute!" and "Look at that!" before he saw the procession marching down the aisle.

What was Kimmie doing here, holding her teddy bear aloft? And Berry, waving her lion and making roaring noises? Around them surged a group of kids: Tina Torres's daughter Anna, Berry's best friend Cindy, Fiona Denny, Brady Franco and a tiny girl who must be his little sister, along with a few children Zack didn't recognize. Each carried a stuffed animal, while behind them Alec Denny's wife, Patty, pulled a plastic wagon filled with more fuzzy creatures. Kate Franco shepherded the children, keeping a close eye on the younger ones, while Bailey brought up the rear with her eleven-month-old twins in a stroller.

His spirits plummeting, Zack figured out this must be the fund-raising scheme the kids had been so excited about. He'd never imagined the animal shelter's future might come at the expense of his patients.

# *Chapter Eighteen*

Jan registered Zack's roller-coaster reactions in her peripheral vision. The past few minutes had been tough on him. And now, just when his cause's triumph seemed certain, he faced a children's crusade.

While he understood how much the shelter meant to the kids, Zack had never wanted pets in the first place. He must be upset they might take precedence over people.

Kimmie had marched onstage alongside Brady as the designated spokeskids, and her heart was shining in her face. To be rejected by her newfound father might cause a long-lasting rift. Fortunately, the choice wasn't his.

The winner, Dr. Rattigan, seemed bemused by the whole proceeding. Even the stern Chandra Yashimoto cracked a smile.

"Save the kitties and puppies!" Kimmie waggled Mischief the bear.

"No more youth in Asia!" Brady shouted. Jan heard chuckles around her at the mispronunciation of *euthanasia*.

"The Aloha Lane Shelter…" Kimmie began.

"Oahu Lane," Brady said.

"The Oahu Lane Shelter needs to fix up their plumbing and stuff."

"Plus build more kennels." Brady hoisted his green dinosaur above his head. "Save the animals!"

The other kids echoed his cry. The crowd clapped and cheered.

"I'm at a disadvantage here," Dr. Rattigan said into the microphone. "I don't have kids or pets. But I do have patients."

Brady scuffed at the stage floor, discouraged. Kimmie stared at the tall man as if her willpower could win the day.

"However, I'd hate to be the most unpopular guy at Safe Harbor," the urologist continued. "So I'm going to hand this hot potato over to the man who deserves this honor as much as I do. Zack Sargent, come on up here!"

Jan caught her breath. Didn't Cole understand he was pitting Zack against his own daughter? Sturdy as she might seem, Kimmie still had only a new and fragile bond with her father.

As Zack mounted the stage, Jan noted the rigidity in his shoulders. This was hard, being put on the spot in front of his colleagues. Not to mention the press and public via the internet.

After the doctors shook hands, Cole left with a light step. Zack gave Kimmie and Brady a tight smile, then faced the room.

"I had no idea they were planning this," he began.

No one stirred, not even Rod Vintner, Jan noted. Kimmie clutched Mischief to her chest.

"I wasn't raised around animals and until recently I didn't allow pets in my house," Zack said. "My daughters and a couple of cats have made some inroads, however."

"Smidge is a kitten," Kimmie corrected. Although only a few feet from her father, she stuck close to Brady. *As if for protection, or am I reading too much into this?* Jan wondered.

"A cat and a kitten," Zack conceded. "As a result of their influence, I visited the Oahu Lane Shelter. I admire their animal-rescue work. It would be a shame if they had to close."

On the stage Dr. T and Dr. Rayburn regarded him speculatively. Chandra Yashimoto stared straight ahead, staying out of it. Wisely, in Jan's opinion.

"Since I'm being asked to display the wisdom of Solomon, I'm going to follow his example and split the money," Zack said. "Not in half, though. I'd like to allocate twenty thousand dollars to repair the shelter's plumbing and air-conditioning systems, and eighty thousand as seed money for a grant program to defray patients' fertility expenses."

Jan felt a weight lift from her. How could anyone disagree with that?

She hadn't considered her daughter's stubbornness. Kimmie's high voice cut through the applause. "No fair! People can earn their own money. Animals don't have a choice. You should give them the whole thing."

Brady poked Kimmie in the side. She ignored him.

Jan saw Bailey and Patty frowning. Kate glanced at Jan apologetically. Apparently none of them had considered they might be sparking a public showdown that could cause real harm.

On the stage, father and daughter formed a study in contrasts. Small, dark-haired and rebellious, Kimmie faced her tall, blond, disapproving father. Their green eyes flared with matching intensity.

Jan knew Zack well enough to read his reaction. He'd been sensible and fair, and Kimmie was too demanding.

Furthermore, his daughter shouldn't be challenging him in front of others.

*Please don't snap at her.*

Much as Jan wished to run up there and pull Kimmie aside, that would only add to the awkwardness. She clamped her lips and waited.

JUST WHEN ZACK HAD started to earn the respect of his co-workers, his seven-year-old daughter was making him look like an idiot. His instincts urged him to put a stop to this now.

Through his mind flashed comments his colleagues had made to or about him. Dr. Rayburn had encouraged him to develop a sense of humor. And when Paige was still single, Zack had heard her tell Nora while she and Zack might be friends, he was too serious for her taste.

In the rear of the auditorium, Rod Vintner rolled his eyes. Trying to figure out why, Zack recalled that once, during a heated discussion, the anesthesiologist had said, "For Pete's sake, lighten up."

*See yourself as others see you.*

It wasn't in Kimmie's power to make a fool of her father—but it was in his own power to do that by over-reacting.

Zack reflected wryly that Berry would have welcomed his compromise with a heartfelt, "Thanks, Daddy!" But Kimmie wasn't Berry.

She was as stubborn as he was—and the way to deal with a stubborn person, as he ought to know, was with reason, not force.

"You can't speak for your whole group," he told her. "Why don't you talk to your friends?"

A flicker of uncertainty broke through her defiance. Brady tipped the scales by saying, "Exactly."

"Okay." Down to floor level Kimmie went, with Brady tagging behind. The children huddled by the stage, whispering urgently. With a grin, Patty lifted a couple of stuffed animals from the wagon and put their fuzzy heads together, too.

"While the children are holding their powwow, let me talk a little about why this grant program is so important." Zack had prepared a statement in case he won. Might as well use it. "Here at Safe Harbor, we aren't just concerned with statistics. We care about individuals and their families."

While the kids continued muttering among themselves, he cited recent advances in surgery and embryology, as well as the upcoming launch of the egg-donor program. When Zack pointed out the price tag for a baby could easily rise to tens of thousands of dollars, many of his colleagues nodded in agreement.

Below, the huddle broke up. Her face set with determination, Kimmie climbed to take her place beside him.

*Please don't let her demand the whole amount.* Zack had no idea how he'd respond to that.

Still, his daughter looked so little and cute he wanted to hug her. Under the circumstances, however, that struck him as disrespectful. "What's your decision?" he asked formally.

Kimmie stood on tiptoe and he lowered the mic to her. "The shelter gets twenty-five thousand. Twenty for the plumbing and five to help with other stuff."

"Done," Zack responded. "Let's shake on it." Solemnly, he held out his hand. As she gripped it the auditorium erupted with approval. The stuffed animals added their happy noises.

Kimmie grinned. "Thanks, Daddy."

Scooping his daughter into his arms, Zack felt as if he'd won a hundred contests.

JAN WAS PROUD OF THEM BOTH. And of Berry, who along with the other children swarmed onto the stage for their share of congratulations.

The excitement lessened only when Chandra Yashimoto arose and moved to the microphone. Although considerably shorter than Zack, she had a commanding presence.

She held up a placard. "Dr. Sargent, it's my honor on behalf of Medical Center Management Inc. to present you with this copy of the winning check. We'll send twenty-five thousand dollars to the Oahu Lane Shelter and the rest to the grant program once a bank account is established."

"Thank you, Ms. Yashimoto." Zack beamed at her and accepted the blown-up image of a check.

"In addition—" from her briefcase, she produced a second placard "—we believe a grant program for fertility patients is such a good idea we're contributing an additional hundred thousand dollars in matching funds. We hope this will encourage the public and corporate donors to support this wonderful project."

Zack nodded gratefully but was unable to speak. Happiness for him swelled inside Jan. What an unexpected vote of confidence.

Dr. Rayburn stepped in, thanking the corporation and assuring everyone that more information would be available shortly on the hospital's website. "We hope to begin accepting patient applications by next summer," he said.

Zack had won. Everyone had won. *Well, not quite.*

After the meeting broke up, Jan said congratulations to Zack and the girls, and waved away the other moms' apologies for springing such a surprise. "It never occurred to me it might backfire," Kate admitted.

"Yeah. Careless of us," Patty chimed in. "Glad it turned out well."

"So am I." Leaving Zack surrounded by well-wishers, Jan excused her way out of the auditorium and retreated to her office.

After what had just happened she loved him more than ever. But she didn't want to live from crisis to crisis. Even though her advice to Dr. Forrest hadn't torpedoed Zack's plans, what if the center *had* survived and the corporation hadn't donated additional funds? She'd still done the right thing by helping Sam.

Thank goodness she didn't have to worry about his relationship with Kimmie. No matter whether they lived in the same house or not, the two would find a way to keep it on solid ground.

Slipping through the door of the outer office, Jan was startled to see Caroline at her desk, typing intently. "I thought you were out sick."

The secretary peered up with red-rimmed eyes. "I promised to finish entering some data for Dr. Rattigan this week. I didn't want to let him down."

Jan had never seen the young woman so subdued. Taking a chair beside the desk, she asked, "What's wrong?"

Caroline stared at the keyboard. "My parents had a big fight last night and my dad moved out."

"I'm sorry." Although reluctant to pry, she asked, "How's your mom taking it?"

"She cried all night. I'm trying to persuade them to get counseling." Caroline took a deep breath. "If my friends saw me like this, they'd get the whole story out of me. It's too personal. Maybe later I can talk about it, but…"

"But having a bunch of people poke into your personal pain makes it worse," Jan said.

"Yeah." The secretary clicked her tongue, as if disgusted with herself. "Is this how you felt about my gossiping? Don't bother to answer. It's obvious."

While this might be an overdue lesson, Jan took no pleasure in the circumstances. "I'm sorry you're going through this."

"You might be living down the street from us," Caroline said. "You'll meet all the neighbors."

"They won't hear a word from me," Jan promised.

"I'm sure the shouting carried down the block." Having relished dishing the dirt on Jan, Caroline seemed hypersensitive to the effects of gossip now. "They might ask you questions."

"They should have better things to do than stick their noses into your family's business," Jan replied. "If not, I'll encourage them to volunteer at the animal shelter. That'll put their time to good use."

Caroline managed a thin smile. "Maybe I'll sign up myself. By the way, what happened with the contest? Or would that be gossiping?"

"Not at all. It's public information." Jan relayed the events of the past hour. Caroline resumed typing in slightly better spirits.

Jan didn't see Zack for the rest of the day. He had patients scheduled, and she was grateful to be busy with her own tasks.

No doubt at dinner they'd celebrate his victory. But while she hated to spoil the mood, tonight she had to explain why she and Kimmie were going to move out.

"I DON'T UNDERSTAND."

All afternoon Zack had been riding high. The estab-

lishment of the grant program came with an unantici-
pated bonus: the respect and approval flowing from his
colleagues had erased his lingering sense of being an
outsider.

A couple of nurses had high-fived him in the hallway.
Dr. Sam had assured him she was thrilled. As for Cole
Rattigan, he'd emailed his thanks for taking him off the
hot seat, adding, "By the way, Jack, I'll never get your
name wrong again."

After dinner Zack had accompanied the girls to Ilsa
Ivy's house, where she'd cried with joy at the good news.
He'd praised both girls equally, and been pleased to see
them giggling and joking on the walk home.

They'd gone upstairs to play an educational video
game. Then Jan quietly took him into the den and dropped
this bombshell.

"Is this because I snapped at you?" Zack couldn't believe she intended to leave after how far they'd come these
past few months, with each other and with the girls. He
loved having his family around, with Jan at the center. "I
already apologized, but I'll do it again. I know I'm unfair
sometimes. Still, I'm learning."

"I can see that." Her mouth quivered.

"Let's at least give this a few more months." Surely
she'd change her mind by then.

Dark hair cascaded over her face as she shook her head.
"I should have told you about Dr. Sam, but the fact is that
around you, I've begun to doubt my own instincts. It feels
like I have to censor myself and that's not right."

"I'm willing to doubt *my* own instincts. It's part of
growing." Zack wasn't giving up without a fight.

"And I'm willing to acknowledge when I'm at fault,"
Jan agreed. "But, Zack, you're more forceful than you realize. Maybe you've got some old anger issues—I don't

mean to psychoanalyze you. It's just that I feel myself becoming more uncertain, like I was years ago. Being willing to fold even when I might be right. I can't truly be myself while I'm living here."

He switched tactics. "Today, Kimmie called me Daddy. She and Berry act more like sisters every day."

"We'll be living less than a mile from here." Jan clenched her hands in her lap. She'd chosen an armchair facing Zack instead of sitting beside him. "Kimmie can come here for overnights, and Berry is welcome to stay with us when you have on-call duty."

He needed a persuasive insight to show they belonged together. Frustrated at not finding one, he blurted, "This is crazy."

"Crazy?" Jan repeated.

Accusing her of being irrational wasn't going to help. "We're a family. I don't expect you to be perfect. I hope you don't expect that of me."

"Certainly not." She stood up. "I love you. I'm sorry I can't live with you." Glancing at her watch, she added, "I'd better go tuck in the girls. We can tell them about this tomorrow."

If she loved him, how could she leave? The irony was infuriating. With an effort, Zack held his peace.

He'd learned to think things over before snapping at her. That was a plus, anyway.

She went upstairs alone. They took turns reading aloud at bedtime so each could bond with both girls. Now they'd be destroying that new tradition along with many more.

Restlessly, Zack wandered into the hall. Upstairs, girl-ish voices echoed as they put on their pajamas and brushed their teeth. Among the chatter he distinctly heard Berry say, "Okay, Mommy."

More proof that Jan belonged here. For heaven's sake, what did she expect from him?

Rather than risk an argument, he went into the kitchen, grabbed his jacket and lifted his car keys from the hook by the garage door. A short drive might help him cool off.

Zack headed north, rolling through side streets. Christmas lights shone from eaves and wound around tree branches. In some yards, displays of Santa Claus and reindeer, nativity scenes or comic-book characters enlivened the darkness.

Aside from a small tree each year Zack had never decorated for the holidays. This year, he'd been thinking it might be fun. But without Jan, the prospect saddened him.

His unplanned path carried him past a small industrial complex. Although the Oahu Lane Shelter sign wasn't lit, his headlights glittered off its reflective paint. The animals would have a merry Christmas, thanks to the children. Despite his initial dismay, Zack was glad they'd stood up for their cause, and that he'd been able to bend.

Damn it, he'd done nothing wrong. Why was Jan punishing him?

The van cruised onward, past yard after yard of homes and trees entwined with colored strands. *Jan and I ought to be buying our own decorations. Going caroling. Planning a special meal.* He'd struggled to make the holidays joyous for Berry since her mother's death, but always there'd been a sense of something missing. How could he have found it—found Jan—only to lose her again?

He had to persuade her to stay.

Ahead, a brightly illuminated yard showed no trace of festivities. In the glare of a portable floodlight a middle-aged man was hauling a large trash bag to a Dumpster, the kind residents borrowed from the city when they had to dispose of extra material. A woman followed, wrinkling her nose as she tossed another bag onto the heap.

With a start Zack recognized the ranch-style house as the place Jan had shown him on her phone. The one she planned to rent. Obviously the owners were clearing it out.

As he rolled past he spotted a familiar figure standing on the sidewalk talking to the woman. Caroline Carter.

To Zack's annoyance she glanced over and gave a start of recognition. Terrific. On Monday it would be all over the hospital that he'd driven past, gaping at Jan's new home like a lovesick teenager.

The receptionist waved him over. Since ignoring her would be pointless Zack pulled to the curb. He lowered the passenger-side window and regarded her questioningly.

"Hi, Dr. Sargent," Caroline said. "What're you doing here?"

"Just driving by." That didn't sound very convincing. "I recognized the place from Jan's photo."

She must have noticed his wary expression, because her next words were, "Don't worry, I'm not going to shoot my mouth off. Didn't Ms. Garcia tell you I learned my lesson?"

*Interesting, if true.* "Must have slipped her mind."

"I can give you a tour," she offered. "Just let me ask the owners."

Zack *was* curious about the place where Jan intended to live. "Sure." He switched off the engine. "That would be great."

Maybe he'd get an idea during the tour. He could sure use some inspiration.

## Chapter Nineteen

Telling Zack about her decision hadn't brought the relief Jan expected. Of course, she'd known it would be a difficult discussion. Still, he'd taken it well. If he'd argued and leveled accusations it would have only confirmed her resolve.

Once the girls were settled she discovered he'd gone out. Easy to understand why. The situation was uncomfortable for them both. Jan regretted springing her news on what should have been a night of celebration, but she had to let him know her decision about the rental.

This house was already full of memories: Thanksgiving, playing with the girls, making love with Zack. If only she didn't feel this underlying anxiety, as if she were a visitor in what should have been her home.

Had a friend asked for advice in such a situation, Jan would have recommended counseling. They could still try that, but only after she left. While she was here the pressure to yield to him in countless ways was too strong.

*It comes from inside me. Does that make it my problem?* There she went, taking the responsibility on herself. Yet he *had* changed.

Jan's footsteps carried her into the living room. As always, the multicolored cushions against the red couch and zebra-striped chairs made her smile. She paused by the photo of Rima.

A warm spirit shone forth. Yet, much as she admired Berry's mother, Jan couldn't help speculating. If Rima hadn't come along would she and Zack have reconciled? Perhaps they'd have matured alongside each other, battling and loving their way to a happy relationship. Or would they have made each other miserable?

Hearing the garage door activate, Jan cut through the dining room into the kitchen. What kind of mood was he in? She knew how easily anger could feed on itself with imagined scenarios and arguments.

The door opened and Zack came through. With a rush she took in the tweed jacket and his dear, woodsy scent. Surprise flickered in his green eyes. "Were you standing here waiting for me?"

Jan chuckled in embarrassment. "I heard the garage open. Guess I just gravitated in this direction."

Zack shrugged off his coat. "There's something I'd like to show you."

"Sure." Despite her light tone she braced for some new attempt to change her mind.

At the table, he produced his phone. Curious, Jan took a chair to his left.

"Oddly enough, I ran into Caroline while I was out," Zack remarked as he clicked some buttons. "I hope she's telling the truth about not gossiping."

"She seems to mean it." The conversation puzzled Jan. "Where did you run into her?"

He held up an image of the house she planned to rent. In the floodlights, Caroline stood in front of a Dumpster. "Lovely view, huh?"

"Charming." Jan waited. Obviously, there must be more.

"I was driving by and saw her talking to the owners. She offered to show me around. Nice place."

"Nothing fancy." Especially not with the trash and smelly dog blankets left by the former renters. Did he mean to muster those as an argument against living there?

"I'd like your opinion of these decorations." He flipped to a shot of a similar house. Green and red lights festooned the eaves and candy canes illuminated the walkway.

"Pretty, I suppose." She wished he'd get to the point.

"How about this?" The next image showed a two-story home engulfed in white lights that also wrapped around several palm trees.

"Overdone. It lacks focus." *Like this presentation.*

"The kids might prefer this one." A large yard displayed Santa's workshop, complete with giant teddy bears.

"Zack, what's this about?"

He set down the phone. "I thought the four of us could decorate both our houses as a family project." He spoke carefully, watching her reaction. "If we pick out the displays and put them up together, it'll help Kimmie and Berry feel like we're still linked. It might bridge the transition."

Did she understand correctly? "It sounds like you're accepting that I'm going to move."

"And offering my assistance, if you want it."

Was there a catch that she'd missed? Jan longed so hard for this decision to be real she couldn't trust it. "Why?"

Zack folded his hands on the table. "While Caroline was showing me through the house, she said something that struck a nerve."

"Caroline did?" The young woman hardly seemed like the type to dazzle one with her insight.

"She said, 'I listened to Ms. Garcia lecture me about gossiping, but until today I never really heard her.'"

Jan was glad her message had been received. "I guess that's because for the first time she might be on the receiving end."

"That made me think about your reasons for leaving. I listened, but I didn't hear you, either." Zack's gaze fixed on hers. "You can't be yourself as long as I insist on controlling you."

"I don't remember using the word *control*."

"My interpretation." He tilted his head. "Am I wrong?"

"No." While Jan hadn't thought of his actions in that light, his analysis rang true.

"Years ago, when I lived with my parents, my dad kept trying to make me over," he said. "The older I got the more it grated. Even after I turned eighteen, he was always evaluating and correcting me, like a principal, with me forever a kid at his school. I wasn't free to explore my own options. I had to live at home during college to save money and it drove me crazy. When I moved out I experienced this wonderful surge of freedom."

"That's right," Jan said in wonder. "You nailed it."

Zack touched her hand. The gentle contact exhilarated her. "It's important that you be happy. I wish you could be happy with me. I love you, Jan. I'd like to be part of your future, but if that means having to co-parent from a distance, then I'll do my best."

"You're letting me go." Sadness warred with a burst of liberation—just as he'd described.

"I have to." He swallowed, and she saw he was holding back a shimmer of tears. "Because I love you that much."

Around her the room sparkled with unusual clarity. Jan noted the buffed golden wood of the cabinets as if for the first time, and the small glass chandelier above the table seemed etched by fairies. "Did the lighting just change in here?"

"Is that a trick question?"

She laughed. "It's gone."

"What is?" He looked as confused as she'd been a few moments ago.

"The weight. The heaviness." She marveled at her sudden buoyancy. "Oh, Zack. That was it."

"Are we talking about Christmas decorations?" he ventured.

"We're talking about us. Being partners. Working as a team, as equals. That's what I couldn't get through to you. I hadn't even articulated it clearly to myself." She supposed he'd always been dominant, in both their perceptions. When she was younger, that had felt natural, but after years of struggle and independence, she'd outgrown her old role.

So, she was thrilled to learn, had he.

"Mind walking me through this?" Zack asked.

"I'd be delighted. I can be myself around you now. You love me enough to accept my decision to leave, if that's what I need."

He touched her cheek. "Dare I hope this means you'll stay?"

Jan nodded, her heart full. "I only needed for you to understand, to truly see things from my point of view. I'll call the rental owners and tell them I'm not taking the house."

He gave her a smile brimming with love. "I hope Caroline won't be disappointed."

"Who'd have imagined she'd turn out to be our fairy godmother?" The idea tickled Jan. "We can tell the girls tomorrow that we're staying. Although I'm not sure exactly how to explain it."

"I am."

"What do you mean?"

To her astonishment he slid off the chair onto one knee. "If you're willing, we can tell them we're getting married. Miss Garcia, will you do me the honor of becoming my wife?" With a trace of uncertainty, he amended, "Unless it's too soon. If this feels like I'm pressuring you…"

"Oh, Zack!" It didn't. Not at all. "Yes. From the minute I saw you again, the first day of school, I knew I still loved you."

"And I fell in love with you all over again," he said.

The next moment she was in his arms, hugging and being hugged. It felt splendidly, magically right.

"And here I thought establishing the grant program was the best thing that could happen to me today," Zack said as they moved into the den to the luxury of the couch. "Thank goodness I got some sense knocked into me."

"If we keep it small, we could get married the weekend after Christmas and have the reception here at the house," Jan mused, her thoughts racing ahead. "If you don't mind?"

"The sooner the better," he murmured.

"I saw the perfect dress in a store the other day and wished I had an excuse to buy it. It's green rather than white. Is that okay?" It was a stunning cocktail-length dress with a short jacket. Exactly the color of his eyes— and Kimmie's.

"Green for the holidays," he murmured approvingly. "But I thought you always dreamed of a big, formal wedding."

That had been a different Jan. "What matters is that everyone we love shares in our special day."

"Let's make sure Berry feels as much a part of things as Kimmie," Zack said.

"Absolutely." Jan snuggled against him. "How about

she gets to be maid of honor in a pretty dress and Kimmie wears a tuxedo as your best…whatever."

She felt his chest shake with laughter. "If they like the idea, fine. And they probably will."

"They'll be adorable." She added teasingly, "Don't forget to hire a photographer."

"An hour ago you were moving out and now we're planning our wedding."

"I waited eight years," Jan responded. "That's long enough."

Placing a finger beneath her chin, Zack tipped her face up and kissed her. For several minutes she thought of nothing but him.

When they came up for air, he said, "Let's go upstairs."

"The girls…"

"Maybe they're asleep."

They went up hand in hand and peeked into the girls' room. Kimmie sprawled on her back in her bed, while Berry curled on her side beneath the princess-style canopy. Each had a cat nestled beside her. Between them, on a small table, rested the book of fairy tales from which Jan had read aloud earlier.

The story had ended with, "And they lived happily ever after." But as she and Zack slipped out, she realized their real story was just beginning.

In his bedroom, he withdrew a velvet jeweler's box from a bureau drawer. "Do you still like these as much as you used to?"

To her astonishment he opened it to reveal a set of elegant rings: the engagement ring she'd thrown at him and the one intended for their wedding day. "You kept them?"

"I guess there was a part of me that never let go."

She slipped on the sparkler. "It's beautiful, and it still fits. I can hardly believe it."

"Start believing." Zack drew her close. "I'm glad it's back where it belongs."

And so, Jan thought, was she. At the start of a wonderful adventure.

Twice upon a time…

*  *  *  *  *

# REQUEST YOUR FREE BOOKS!
## 2 FREE NOVELS PLUS 2 FREE GIFTS!

## LOVE, HOME & HAPPINESS

**YES!** Please send me 2 FREE Harlequin® American Romance® novels and my 2 FREE gifts (gifts are worth about $10). After receiving them, if I don't wish to receive any more books, I can return the shipping statement marked "cancel." If I don't cancel, I will receive 4 brand-new novels every month and be billed just $4.49 per book in the U.S. or $5.24 per book in Canada. That's a saving of at least 14% off the cover price! It's quite a bargain! Shipping and handling is just 50¢ per book in the U.S. and 75¢ per book in Canada.* I understand that accepting the 2 free books and gifts places me under no obligation to buy anything. I can always return a shipment and cancel at any time. Even if I never buy another book, the two free books and gifts are mine to keep forever.

154/354 HDN FEP2

Name _____ (PLEASE PRINT) _____

Address _____ Apt. # _____

City _____ State/Prov. _____ Zip/Postal Code _____

Signature (if under 18, a parent or guardian must sign) _____

### Mail to the **Reader Service:**
### IN U.S.A.: P.O. Box 1867, Buffalo, NY 14240-1867
### IN CANADA: P.O. Box 609, Fort Erie, Ontario L2A 5X3

Not valid for current subscribers to Harlequin American Romance books.

### Want to try two free books from another line?
### Call 1-800-873-8635 or visit www.ReaderService.com.

* Terms and prices subject to change without notice. Prices do not include applicable taxes. Sales tax applicable in N.Y. Canadian residents will be charged applicable taxes. Offer not valid in Quebec. This offer is limited to one order per household. All orders subject to credit approval. Credit or debit balances in a customer's account(s) may be offset by any other outstanding balance owed by or to the customer. Please allow 4 to 6 weeks for delivery. Offer available while quantities last.

**Your Privacy**—The Reader Service is committed to protecting your privacy. Our Privacy Policy is available online at www.ReaderService.com or upon request from the Reader Service.

We make a portion of our mailing list available to reputable third parties that offer products we believe may interest you. If you prefer that we not exchange your name with third parties, or if you wish to clarify or modify your communication preferences, please visit us at www.ReaderService.com/consumerchoice or write to us at Reader Service Preference Service, P.O. Box 9062, Buffalo, NY 14269. Include your complete name and address.

HAR11B

*What happens when a Texas nanny learns she is
the biological daughter of a prince? Her rancher boss
steps in to help protect her from the paparazzi, but who
can protect her from her attraction to him?*

*Read on for an excerpt of
A HOME FOR NOBODY'S PRINCESS
by* USA TODAY *bestselling author Leanne Banks.*

*Available October 2012*

"This is out of control." Benjamin sighed. "Well, damn.
I guess I'm gonna have to be your fiancé."

Coco's jaw dropped. "What?"

"It won't be real," he said quickly, as much for himself
as for her. After the debacle of his relationship with Brooke,
the idea of an engagement nearly gave him hives. "It's just
for the sake of appearances until the insanity dies down.
This way it won't look like you're all alone and ready to have
someone take advantage of you. If someone approaches
you, then they'll have to deal with me, too."

She frowned. "I'm stronger than I seem," she said.

"I know you're strong. After what you went through for
your mom and helping Emma to settle down, I know you're
strong. But it's gotta be damn tiring to feel like you've
always got to be on guard."

Coco sighed and her shoulders slumped. "You're right
about that." She met his gaze with a wince. "Are you sure
you don't mind doing this?"

"It's just for a little while," he said. "You mentioned that
a fiancé would fix things a few minutes ago. I had to run it
through my brain. It seems like the right thing to do."

She gave a slow nod and bit her lip. "Hmm. But it would cut into your dating time."

Benjamin laughed. "That's not a big focus at the moment."

"It would be a huge relief for me," she admitted. "If you're sure you don't mind. And we'll break it off the second you feel inconvenienced."

"No problem," he said. "I'll spread the word. Should be all over the county by lunchtime. No one can know the truth. That's the only way this will work."

Coco took a deep breath and closed her eyes as if preparing to take a jump into deep water. "Okay" she said, and opened her eyes. "Let's do it."

*Will Coco be able to carry out the charade?*

*Find out in Leanne Banks's new novel—*
*A HOME FOR NOBODY'S PRINCESS.*

*Available October 2012 from Harlequin® Special Edition®*

# SPECIAL EDITION

**Life, Love and Family**

## Sometimes love strikes in the most unexpected circumstances...

Soon-to-be single mom Antonia Wright isn't looking
for romance, especially from a cowboy. But when
rancher and single father Clayton Traub rents a room
at Antonia's boardinghouse, Wright's Way, she isn't
prepared for the attraction that instantly sizzles between
them or the pain she sees in his big brown eyes.
Can Clay and Antonia trust their hearts and build the
family they've always dreamed of?

### Don't miss

# THE MAVERICK'S READY-MADE FAMILY

## by Brenda Harlen

*Available this October from Harlequin® Special Edition®*

www.Harlequin.com

HSE65697

## HARLEQUIN Romance

At their grandmother's request, three estranged
sisters return home for Christmas to the small town
of Beckett's Run. Little do they know that this family
reunion will reveal long-buried secrets…
and new-found love.

Discover the magic of Christmas in a brand-new
Harlequin® Romance miniseries.

In October 2012, find yourself
### SNOWBOUND IN THE EARL'S CASTLE
by **Fiona Harper**

Be enchanted in November 2012 by a
### SLEIGH RIDE WITH THE RANCHER
by **Donna Alward**

And be mesmerized in December 2012 by
### MISTLETOE KISSES WITH THE BILLIONAIRE
by **Shirley Jump**

**Available wherever books are sold.**

celebrating 15 YEARS

*Love Inspired*

The rancher meets his match this Christmas…

Be enchanted this season by author

# Pamela Tracy

Raising three sons and running his ranch keeps single dad
Jared McCreedy busy from sunup to sundown. Becoming
involved with feisty single mom Maggie Tate is not on his
to-do list. But he needs her help dealing with his youngest
son's learning problem. Like Jared, Maggie doesn't want any
romantic complications in her life…especially with a man
who makes her temper flare—and her pulse race. The risk
of opening her heart is too great for her to chance. Then
again, it *is* the season for faith and miracles….

# Once Upon a Christmas

*Available October 2012 wherever books are sold!*